THE SEER
AND OTHER STORIES

FOREST BOOKS

JONAS LAURITZ IDEMIL LIE was born in November 1833 at Hokksund, Biker, near Drammen. When he was about five years old his family moved to Tromsø, where he started school in 1838. In 1846 his family moved south, to near Bergen, and Lie finished his schooling there. He studied at the university in Kristiania from 1851 to 1858, where he graduated in Law: while at university he met, amongst others, Ibsen, Bjørnson and Vinje.

His first publication was a collection of poems, *Digte*, in 1866. But his literary breakthrough really came with the publication in 1870 of *Den Fremsynte, eller Billeder fra Nordland* (The Seer). The book was an immediate success in Norway, something which was extremely unusual for a début author.

From 1871 to 1905 Lie lived almost exclusively abroad: during this time he wrote over twenty novels, plays and stories, establishing himself as one of the greats of Norwegian literature.

Lie returned to Norway in 1905. Two years later his wife, Thomasine, died, and Lie died the following year, in 1908.

BRIAN MORTON was born in Paisley and brought up in the West of Scotland. After graduating from the University of Edinburgh, he researched and taught at the University of East Anglia. In 1979, he was visiting lecturer at the University of Tromsø, Norway. He is currently literary editor of *The Times Higher Education Supplement*.

RICHARD TREVOR was born in Zambia on 26th February 1964. In 1977 the family moved to Scotland and in 1983 he went to Aberdeen University to read Norwegian and Russian, graduating in 1988 with an M.A. (Hons). During his university studies he went on an eight-month visit to Tromsø and discovered Lie's novel *The Seer*. Having started translating the first chapter only as a challenging exercise, he then found himself compelled to go on and eventually, having worked through many of the long winter nights, he succeeded in finishing it. He married Uta in 1987 and they now live in Switzerland.

Jonas Lie

The
SEER
& Other Stories

FOREST
BOOKS
London & Boston

*Translated from
the Norwegian by*
**Brian Morton &
Richard Trevor**

PUBLISHED BY
FOREST BOOKS

20 Forest View, Chingford, London E4 7AY, U.K.
61 Lincoln Road, Wayland, MA 01778, U.S.A.

First published 1990

Cover painting © Theodor Kittelsen
Cover design © Ann Evans
The Seer translation © Richard Trevor
Introduction and translation of other stories © Brian Morton

ISBN NO. 0 948259 65 5

British Library Cataloguing in Publication Data
Lie, Jonas, 1833–1908
The seer and other Norwegian stories.
I. Title
839.823 [F]

Library of Congress Catalog Card No.
90–80376

Forest Books gratefully acknowledge the support of
NORLA (Norwegian Literature Abroad)

Printed in Great Britain by BPCC Wheatons Ltd, Exeter

Cover painting: *Draugen* by Theodor Kittelsen, National Gallery, Oslo.

Contents

Introduction

'Nothing seemed on the face of things less propitious than that a one-time successful and even wealthy lawyer, approaching middle age, should take to writing fiction with the immediate aim of making enough money to pay back his creditors': not Sir Walter Scott, to whom James McFarlane's words almost equally apply, but the Norwegian novelist Jonas Lie. Lie was born almost exactly a year after Scott's death, but their careers seem curiously in parallel. Both men were trained in the law; both took to fiction writing relatively late in life and to mitigate crippling debt; both were obsessed to the point of possession by a childhood landscape; both were instrumental in establishing the international literary signature of their respective countries. Both are easily and frequently underestimated.

Just as it is now impossible to regard Scott as an unquestioning apologist for a social and political status quo, it is ironic that the work which established Lie's reputation is, in many respects, his least characteristic; as McFarlane puts it, 'Those qualities which made Lie immediately popular in the [18]70s and [18]80s have little to do with his real and considerable merit'. He became known in Norway as *hjemmenes dikter*, 'the poet of the hearth', and was valued primarily for his exact rendition of social life, an impressionism that seemed to lend itself to sharp, static images and set-pieces rather than to powerful narrative or moral and psychological penetration; Lie himself frequently uses the analogy of painting — as does the later, but very similar, Cora Sandel — but he makes it clear that his images always serve 'the peculiar mental composition of the hero'. He shares with Scott a profound conviction that literary landscape is never neutral and external set-dressing, but that it is deeply inscribed in both character and language. Though he turned away from it in life and in imagination, Lie could never shake himself free of the ambiguities of Nordland.

Lie was born on 6 November 1833, at Hougsund, Eker, near Kristiania (present-day Oslo). At the age of five, he made the most significant transition of his life, when the family moved to the northern provincial capital of Tromsø. His earliest recorded ambition was, oddly, to become a gunsmith (the same wish surfaces in the character of Jorgen in Lie's 1883 novel *The Family at Gilje*) and he showed little sign of adolescent bookishness. Nonetheless he was, by his own admission, a 'twilight nature', deeply impressionable and Tromsø overwhelmed him with what Alrik Gustafson calls 'its kaleidoscopic shifting of landscape effects, its lurid intensities of light and darkness, its eternal night of winter and continuous day of summer, its fantastic world of darksome superstitions'.

Though heredity is no more convincing a formula for literary nature than geography, Lie inherited a significant tinge of Finnish (and probably gipsy) blood from his mother. His magistrate father was an altogether more prosaic nature and sent the painfully shortsighted teenager off to the notoriously toughening Naval Academy. Against all physical and intellectual odds Lie qualified as a lawyer and found work in a government office. He dabbled in verse and, more insidiously, in timber futures. In 1868, the bottom fell out of the lumber business and he found himself in serious debt. It isn't clear to what extent he did use writing royalties to repay his creditors (as Scott did so scrupulously and self-destructively) and McFarlane is almost certainly right in stressing that the financial debacle acted on Lie as a 'mechanism of release'. By forcing him to write, it forced him to confront aspects of his experience and nature that had been buried by education and law-work. Lie was a dilettante poet, as Scott was not, and his literary debut all the more remarkable for its suddenness.

When *Den Fremsynte (The Seer)* appeared in 1870, Lie was 37. Its success changed the direction of his life at a stroke, not least in that he was to spend relatively little of the remainder of it — he died in 1908 — in Norway. The next three decades saw Lie and his wife living in Rome, Bavaria and Paris, where he was lionised by *Figaro* and *Revue des Deux Mondes* as one of the burgeoning generation of Scandinavian modernists. Lie was neither as fiercely nationalistic as Bjørnstjerne Bjørnson (they clashed later over the older Bjørnson's political activities), nor as instinctively cosmopolitan as Henrik Ibsen, but he was quintessentially Nordic and thus an object of fascination. Whether his instincts were immediately attuned to fiction-writing is a matter of some doubt. It is clear now that he was very dependent on the editorial judgement of both Bjørnson and Thomasine Lie; his wife edited and reduced the text considerably and may even have censored, consciously or not, some of its worst excesses. *The Seer* succeeded — and succeeds — almost despite itself. Its contemporary reputation was founded almost entirely on Lie's ability to register local colour and custom rather than on its visionary material. By conventional standards, it is very nearly clumsy, too dependent on 'found' narrative sources. It recalls — not altogether to its own advantage — the complex narrative and structural devices of James Hogg's *The Private Memoirs and Confessions of Justified Sinner*, but without Hogg's virtuoso handling and moral ambivalence.

The visionary David Holst is nonetheless a powerful creation and the framing narrative is prosaic to a purpose, for Lie was not yet ready to explore the darker regions of his imagination. In the years that followed, he turned out a stream of novels that, while far from representative of his true genius, displayed a growing professionalism. Unlike the mainstream of Scandinavian writers of the 1870s and 1880s, Lie was not primarily a 'social' novelist, concerned with the identification and rectification of society's problems. Because Lie was concerned with deeper human anomalies, his true literary-historical location is closer to what we know as Modernism. For two decades after his remarkable debut, his imagination seems to have marked (very lucrative) time. The novels of the middle years — *Tremastern 'Fremtiden'/The Barque 'Future'* (1872), *Lødson og hans Hustru/The Pilot and his Wife* (1874), *Rutland* (1880), *Gaa Paa!/Go On!* (1882), *Familjen paa Gilje/ The Family at Gilje* (1883), and *Kommandørens Døtre/The Commodore's Daughters* (1886) — are almost *too* well constructed too forensic and exact, and too dependent, again, on exactly rendered portraits of bourgeois life.

In 1880 Lie had written 'It is part of my observation of life — this discrepancy between intellectual development and moral ignorance that can manifest itself in one and the same person. Passion, this wild beast within man, breaks out the moment he least expects it; for he is not practised in controlling it.' Ten years further on, and now two full decades after his fictional debut, *Onde Magter/Evil Powers* marked a sudden darkening of his vision. In it he speculated 'Might there not be a little, exciting and incalculable troll concealed somewhere deep within.' It's no accident that psychoanalysis took early and deep root in Scandinavia; the emotional and cultural apparatus was already in place in the work of Lie and Ibsen and Strindberg.

Lie's 'trolls' correspond in large part to what Freud was to identify as unconscious impulses. They are 'oceanic' and atavistic, capricious and disruptive. 'That there are Trolls in human beings everyone knows who has an eye for that kind of thing. They lie within the personality and bind it like the immovable part of a mountain, like a capricious sea and uncontrollable weather. Trolldom lives . . . inside mankind as temperament, natural will, explosive power.' Hindsight primed to detect 'that kind of thing' reveals that the bland surface of Lie's middle novels is thinner than is immediately apparent; something is held in check, often at the cost of unfettered feeling.

In 1891 and 1892, Lie published two extraordinary volumes of stories, prefaced with what amounted to a statement of belief. Along with *The Seer*, *Trold* and *Trold: ny samling* constitute his most remarkable work. The two volumes of *Trolls* are like nothing else he wrote. They represent first of all a drastic simplification and purification of style; where *The Seer* — like *Wuthering Heights*, *The Great Gatsby*, Hogg's *Justified Sinner*, and other visionary works — was filtered through a haze of sceptical or 'editorial' discourse, in *Trolls* Lie confronted his unconscious head-on. The stories draw extensively from folk-material and almost certainly Lie was aware of the series of *Norske Folkeeventry/Norwegian Folk Stories* edited from 1842 by Asbjørnsen and Moe. Writing of the late stories, Gustafson says 'some of them [are] told in the straightforward unadorned narrative manner of the original folk tale, others conceived in the profoundly lyric vein of the best of romantic nature mysticism, and still others written with an obvious and immediate moral purpose'; most often, though, all three elements are discernible simultaneously, and that is Lie's great achievement.

The underlying 'moral pupose', whatever variations are wrought upon it in individual stories, is a need for (eventual) accommodation and restraint, a rite of passage that restores to the protagonist a 'healthy' balance of drives. Like Freud and Scott, Lie was basically a conservative, but one who accepted the dramatic risk of moral chaos; Lie's sea settings would have struck a chord even in the land-locked Austrian, for whom the ocean was the profoundest image of our unconscious life. Whether they would have agreed on the manner of attaining safe harbour is less obvious. In his introduction to *Trolls*, Lie stated his belief that 'Penitence is mankind's first step in his desire to separate himself from and lift himself above the elemental powers, and is followed by all kinds of magic and mediatory means to force the elemental power down ... how far this stage of Trolldom follows mankind even into civilized life might be a very useful and instructive demonstration — perhaps also somewhat astonishing. The fear of existence, the great unknown about us, which is also the foundation of our religious feeling, constantly shifts its form and name according to the various levels of enlightenment. It lives in the mystical experimentalist as table-turning, spirit-rapping and such, in the learned under high-sounding scentific conditions such as the 'fourth dimension' which in the past has in a sense been the lumber-closet into which man puts all of that which he cannot explain to himself.'

The great achievement of *Trolls* is that, whatever the reader's presumed level of enlightenment, it is never absolutely certain just how much belief requires to be suspended in order to follow the narrative. Are his sea-ghosts real, or fables, or psychological projections? It is part of Lie's genius that his most outlandish creations manage to survive even the most robustly enquiring logic.

He is a conservative, but he is also an optimist and by no means a nostalgic reactionary. His last great book, published in 1901, was *Naar Jernteppet falder/When the Iron Curtain Falls*. It concerns a party of civilized people on a transatlantic liner who suddenly learn that a huge bomb is on board, primed to destroy them. Their reactions are extreme, but also profoundly therapeutic, for when they realise that the bomb has been a false alarm, they are transformed, raised to a new level of enlightenment, and they reach land as a group of moral penitents, freed, as Lie would free us all, of their trolls.

Brian Morton

The Seer

(or *Pictures from Nordland*)

Translated by Richard Trevor

Translator's Note

This translation is based on the last edition of *Den Fremsynte* that Lie approved, the 1903 edition. I have retained Lie's occasionally idiosyncratic spelling of place-names. A number of words or references peculiar to nineteenth-century Norway have been included in a glossary at page 94.

For their help and encouragement in this translation, I should like to thank Irene Scobbie, Jo Eggen and the staff at Tromsø University.

Dedicated with love to Uta.

R.T.

Introduction

I know many people who have had the same desire that sometimes overcomes me, precisely to choose a storm to go for a walk in. They are mostly people who, from a childhood in the open air in the countryside, have gone over to occupations which entail sitting still, and for whom the living-room sometimes becomes too cramped and uncomfortable — or of course poets. Their memories and imaginations live, more or less unknown to themselves, in a steady longing to get away from the stuffy indoors and life in a tenement-house in town.

When the countryside then comes into the city one day in the form of a real rainstorm, shaking the tiles and now and then hurling one at you, whilst the streets turn to canals, the corners to ambushes where a whirlwind falls upon one's umbrella and after a more or less protracted, deft struggle, twists and tears it until in the end one is left with just the stick and the skeleton — then it happens now and again that a quiet, worthy civil servant or businessman, after the day's toil in the office, instead of sitting at home as usual in the afternoon in his comfortable living-room says to his wife that he 'unfortunately has to go into town for a while'. And the reason that he unfortunately has to go out is, naturally, 'business'. How little would it become a staid, ponderous man, who is perhaps a provost or one of the town's elders, to admit, if only to himself, that he is childish enough to walk about fantasizing in storms, and that he only wanted to go down to the jetty to see the foam spraying over the slipway and the ships in the harbour toying with disaster. He must naturally have something to do out there — if nothing else then at least, broadly speaking, to see to it that not '*quid detrimenti capiat respublica*'; which is to say that the town, whose welfare he in one way or another has to attend to, does not blow down.

3

The thing is, there is revolution on the streets — not a political one, God preserve him from participating in suchlike — but one of those which in its way attracts him because it stirs up a revolt in all of his old memories, and in which he shamefully enough contrives to participate, even although in its manner it storms all Police regulations, breaks windows, quenches lights, tears tiles from the houses, breaks jetties and mooring arrangements and chases policemen and watchmen into their holes.

It is nature's loud battle-cry, right in the middle of the civilised city, to all of his childhood memories, to his imagination and feeling for nature, which he obeys like an old bugle-horse that hears the signal of its youth and suddenly leaps over the fence.

After a couple of hours' walking out in the weather the fire in his blood is abated, and home comes the same quiet, ponderous man, who *carefully* puts his stick and galoshes aside in their usual places in the hall and is nagged by his wife, who has been concerned about him and now relieves him of his wet clothes. He himself is, strangely enough, despite his hardships in an excellent mood that same evening, and has so exceedingly many things to relate about the storm — all things which are fitting, naturally, in the guise of concern that damage might be caused or that fire might break out in the town that very evening.

It was in such a storm that I — who am a practising physician and who thus have justifiable grounds, both for my own part and for others', for being out in town at all hours of day and night — one rain-, mist- and storm-filled October afternoon was out roaming the streets of Kristiania and took pleasure in letting the weather lash me in the face, whilst my good raincoat for the remainder protected my person.

Darkness had gradually set in, and the lighted gas-lamps flickered in the gusts of wind, so that I came to think of lighthouses on a misty night out on the coast. Now and again an unlocked door would swing open and shut with a crash like a distress shot. My silent observation in this connection was that even now, in our nervous times, there must be found a surprising number of people without nerves, for such crashes thunder through the whole building right up to the attic, opening and shutting, shutting and opening: the blast fills the passages and doors spring open; it is unpleasant for everyone, but no-one bothers to go down to shut the source of the evil; the doorman is out in town and the domestic well-being might as well be gone too, then.

It was just such an unlocked, untiringly slamming door that became the entrance to what I here have to relate.

For as I walked past it I heard a voice that seemed very well known to me, an old, dear voice — although at first I did not know whence I remembered it — calling impatiently for the doorman.

It was about the swinging door. Clearly he was the only nervous individual in the building; in any case the doorman was not one, for he appeared to be equally unfeeling both towards his door and towards the man who was attending to it, and who was vainly trying with a door-key which did not appear to fit.

Eventually the doorman came out of his underground hole, and it was during the little altercation which developed between the now conciliatory and gentle voice, afraid of its own irritability, and the growling doorman, that with all the power of an awakening memory I recognised before me my old friend from my student days, David Holst, with whom I had lived three of the richest years of my youth.

'If that's you, David, then let me in before you close up!' I called, just as I would have done in the good old days, twenty years ago.

The door opened wide, and a squeeze of the hand by the dim shape that had stepped out told me that *he* had not needed to root in the depths of his memory for as long as I had in mine, but that he had remembered me thence at once.

'Follow me!' were his only words, and thus we climbed silently, he in front and I behind, up through the unlit flights of stairs, one, two, three floors, and even one considerably narrower stair higher. There he took me by the hand, something which was certainly required, since, as far as I could make out, the way led in across an upper loft with clothes lines hanging in it — he also bade me bow my head.

On the way I had my doubts.

His hand — I came to remember that in the old days he was somewhat vain about it — was clammy, probably from agitation, and he stopped sometimes on the stairs as if he had to catch his breath. The cramped upper loft stair also whispered to me that my friend David, who in his time had certainly had the promise of a good head, could not have made much worldly progress with it.

He opened a door and bade me enter first.

On a longish table stood a lamp whose shade abruptly limited its illumination, to only about a foot-and-a-half around the lampbase, onto an inkstand and some papers that lay there, so that to begin with the extremities of the table appeared to me to lie in darkness. Behind it there seemed to me to be something like a black grave, but which a little later, when the eye became accustomed to the lamp's steep lighting, turned out to be a sofa, before which there stood a nearly equally-long, painted worktable with squared ends.

When two people who have been friends in their youth meet in such a way, there is often beneath their straightforward manner still a secret bashfulness to conquer; there is a layer of many years of differing experience which has to be cleared aside.

After a little pause, my friend, as if with a sudden resolution, quickly moved up and took the lampshade off, so that it grew light throughout the room.

'You see,' he said, 'things are just the way they used to be in the old days with me, only that there are now two skylights instead of one, several more shelves of books and a slightly better monthly wage, which I get by combining a teaching position at one of the alms-schools here with a not very difficult post on a newspaper. That is really everything I need, you see. I first moved in here this spring from Bergen and should really have called on you, but still haven't got around to it; on the street you have always seemed preoccupied to me, as if you were dashing to your practice. But now that I've got you in my garret we'll have a chat about old times, and how things are with you. Take off your coat, and I shall go down in the meantime and see about getting together some toddy.'

With that he replaced the lampbowl and disappeared out of the door.

This, my friend's somewhat forced introductory speech, did not seem quite natural to me; it was as if, with his sweeping confidence, he were conforming more to my than to his own character, and altogether it gave me the impression he wanted to ward off any unnecessary questions in advance.

We had, after all, still not exchanged as much as a handshake, and I in any case had not said a syllable, indeed I had really not seen more of him yet than that little glimpse of his face, just as he turned towards the lamp and replaced the shade.

I recognised, however, despite the difference in age, that same

6

lean, fine, pale face, which in the old days could sometimes acquire such a beautiful, melancholy expression — it was thus that he remained forever photographed in my memory — but his features had now acquired a striking sharpness, and in the short glance which I caught was an expression simultaneously suffering and wary which caused me an indescribable pain.

I have seen patients give me that same look when they were afraid that my intention was to operate on them and I thought now to understand at least this much from it: that, insofar as operating was involved here, it was on my friend's old confidence — besides which that this would require all of my skill.

I was once the most trusting fellow under the sun, but since I became a physician and have seen what people really are like, and that there is nothing in the whole world that one should not presume, even of the best of people, if one is not to misdiagnose the cause of the illness, I have been converted to an absolutely suspicious person.

I suspect everything and everyone, even those worthy men who take walks out in storms.

A Red Indian does not steal more unnoticed or silently through the densest forest than I, when I am pressed to it, steal into my patient's confidence, and it was as if my friend David had all at once become a patient to me. Now he would hardly draw me off any longer with his talk of 'old times' and with a glass of punch in his 'unchanged student garret'.

My first strategem was now in haste to continue my review of the room, which my friend somewhat fleetingly had let me begin. I took the lamp and set about looking around.

Beside the wall opposite the sofa, under the ceiling which was slanted due to the roof, was his bed, with a small round table before it. On a bookcase which stood on the floor up against the wall, in the corner at the foot of the bed, I recognised the bust of Henrik Wergeland, the chin and nose even more defective than in my time, and now in addition blinded in one eye; it had gone nearly as badly with him as with the old meerschaum pipe which I used to smoke, and which I had also recognised, despite its having been thoroughly hewn and gashed in all directions.

My friend had, to wit, the habit of sitting and incising his lines of thought in it whilst he smoked tobacco and now and again tossed a word into the conversation, to keep it going, as one tosses fuel onto a fire — it was somehow more the mood of the talk, and the fact above all that there was talk, than the thought itself that he was concerned about. And in that position he would often have precisely that still, melancholy expression about him, as if he were smiling at something beautiful which we others did not see.

Between the bed and the bookcase I discovered several bottles, plain wine bottles, and with the speed of lightning the suspicion flashed into my mind — I have, as I said, not by nature but through disappointment become the incarnate suspiciousness — that my friend must have fallen to drink.

I put the lamp aside on the floor. In one bottle was ink, in another paraffin and in the third, smaller, codliver oil, which he must have been taking, presumably for his chest.

I recalled the clammy hand, his pauses and heavy breathing on the stair, and felt ashamed, a proper wretch, I who could have thought my youth's dear friend — and, I might well say, mentor — on a level with any other common scoundrel, who without a doubt should be suspected.

In silence he was given my contrite apology, whilst I read across the titles on the spines and recognised a few of the books. This seemed to be none other than his student bookcase. I withdrew a thick book, old *Saxo Grammaticus*, which I remembered once having bought at an auction and presented to him, but now I found something quite different to think about.

For me, it was like being someone who draws a brick from a wall and suddenly finds a secret entrance — I felt that I was all at once before the entrance to my friend's secret, even although still only before a deep, dark room, through which the imagination might well roam, but into which I in reality could not see, even had my friend himself handed me the light.

The thing which to that degree attracted my attention and which, as it were, nailed all of my senses and memories to the spot, was no hole, but the head of a violin, which stuck up behind the bookcase with a dusty neck and a tangle of strings between the pegs.

A slack bass string hung down; the overstretched, snapped discant had curled itself upwards, and beneath the two whole strings, as I confirmed for myself by feel and by taking further books from the row, the bridge lay flat. I investigated the violin, which I could not well remove, just as carefully as if I had found a friend ill and famished — there was an unrepaired split in its front. Caught up in old memories, I could not prevent that I became tuned to a melancholy, such a melancholy mood.

I closed up my hold of books, placed the lamp back on the table and myself in the sofa, where, with the puffing meerschaum — I saw amongst other things my own initials, carved by myself — I gave myself up to reminiscences which I wish to share here, despite the danger that the reader might find that my friend stays away rather a long time with the punch. Through them, he will become close in a way that he was to *my* soul, in the light of the memories of my youth, and in a way that the reader must know him, with me, if he is to be able to understand him.

Our student acquaintanceship arose naturally from the fact that we were Nordlanders both.

He was three or four years older than I, and his being the trusted, although anonymous theatre critic in the journal *H* . . . in itself gave him, moreover, an official superiority in my eyes, to which I bowed.

But more than this his mien impressed itself on my youthful power of imagination. There was something unusually noble about his slender figure and his fine, narrow, serious face, with that high brow and that great, curly, black mass of hair at the temples. The strong eyebrows and a pronounced Roman nose somehow drew one's attention from his eyes, which were light blue and more in keeping with his paleness and his beardless face than with the more energetic part of his features. It was, after all, these latter that gave one's first impression of him. Later I learnt to read his features differently and to see that precisely in them lay engraved the confluence of that double nature in which his life was gradually ground asunder.

A fine smile when he spoke and a reserved manner lent him a certain distinction, which certainly greatly impressed me.

He was the only student I knew who did not wear a 'student's cap' — he wore a flat, blue seaman's cap with a short brim, which suited him very well.

When he grew excited, which could happen to him in a dispute, for he was a sorely strong logician — something, though, into which he only put his intellect, but as far as I know never really his heart or his deeper feelings — his voice would not be up to it: it became overstrained and shrill, as from a poor chest. Such a

9

recontre would always affect him, too, and would leave him in an irritable unease for a long time afterwards.

An idiosyncracy of his was that he sometimes took himself off on long walks, lasting several days, out in the countryside, and this both summer and winter. He would never hear of any company. Had he wished it, he would have turned to me — I felt that — and it could therefore never occur to me to press myself on him.

He would leave without a knapsack at such times; this I noticed once when by chance I saw him crossing the fields nearly twenty miles from town, where I was on a visit.

When he came home again he was always in the best of moods, whilst on the contrary, before he left he was always taciturn and melancholy, so that I had to provide for the conversation almost all by myself. He was like that, with moody periods.

A mark that such a frame of mind had set in was, for me, that very violin that I now twenty years later found stringless, hidden behind his bookcase.

As it lay there, for me it was again the same mark, although now no longer of a period of days, but of years.

This violin he had once held in high esteem, it had had the place of honour on his wall with the bow at its side. He had been given it by a friend, an old sacristan from his home up in Nordland who had taught him to play, and who had apparently been a sort of musical genius of the kind who never achieve what they should in this world.

David very much liked to fantasize, not just *on* this violin — he had a fine ear for music and had learnt not a little — but also *about* it: where it originally harked from, and how old it could be? He would most willingly interpret an unclear stamp in the inside as meaning that it 'was possibly a *Cremona*'; he was a little partial on this point, and for him that room for guessing was obviously a glory of the violin.

David Holst had something which he called classicial music, a couple of longer items which he played from scores. This used to appeal to me rather less and always seemed to me to be in keeping with what was foremost in his bearing when he was behaving as a logician. It was more like a strict mental school-rote — and to be sure he would play quite correctly then, as he would otherwise write or dispute — than like something heartfelt.

Those times, when classical music and critical conversation

reigned in the garret, were surely the ones in which he himself felt most in equilibrium. He was also less sincere in his bearing then, even towards me.

But then there came times when the music stand would rest in the corner.

He might sit for long periods and stare into the distance, as if he had fallen deep into thought, and then air his mood on his violin in all sorts of fantasies, which in a completely different way than his so-called classical music appealed to my not very tuned ear.

They were all sorts of small pieces, which gradually would be drawn more and more into his own minor mood, and sometimes a strangely mournful melody, which I did actually only hear him play right through some few times, and then always as in a kind of oblivion.

I had on these occasions a feeling, as if he were entrusting something delightful to me which he had lost in his life and which should ever be mourned.

Further into such a period he became, as I have said, more irregular, and was seldom to be found at home; sometimes he might even ironise bitterly about comrades, professors and circumstances then, and his target would emerge well-nigh bloodied.

I used to have the privilege of taking the key and going into my friend's room, even when he was not home. If his violin hung untended I knew that things were bad, and that his own condition would approximately match that of the violin. The first thing he would do when all was well again was indeed always carefully put it in order.

Never had I in that time, however, seen this apple of his eye so abandoned and treated as I now, twenty years later, found it again: dusty and split, behind the bookcase.

That I thereby acquired melancholy thoughts and thus suspected a not very cheerful life story, the reader will now to some extent be able to understand, and thus hopefully forgive me for having taken him with me from David Holst's room, where I was sitting waiting for him to return with the punch, so deep into the land of my youth's memories.

For three years we had been together almost daily. Afterwards, David Holst had to go out as a tutor, and our ways separated, as is wont to happen in life.

Here, this evening, was to be the meeting place.

11

There was a chinking out in the passage, and a little later David Holst carefully opened the door for a maid, who brought in a steaming jug with the relevant appurtenances, which could well be to the taste of a man who, as I this afternoon, had been out and about in a storm for many hours.

David found me installed on his sofa with his pipe in my mouth and his slippers on my feet, exactly as things would have been between us in the old days — and this I now reckoned in silence as one of my cunning wiles; for by these tokens, his pipe and slippers, I without further ado presumed us to be on our old, intimate footing.

I felt as though I were a commander-in-chief who is lucky enough to be able to open the battle by immediately occupying a whole province.

In the absence of his usual place on the sofa, David pushed a chair up to the table, and sat directly opposite me, as the punch tray was placed between us.

Now we again both sat at the brink of that same pool of happiness, in which we had tumbled in our youth so many times; but now we both dipped more carefully.

In the course of the conversation he often leant over towards me, as if he were listening, and his head thus came within the compass of the lamp's strong illumination.

I noticed then that his hair had become very thin and somewhat flecked with grey, and that small pearls of sweat stood out on his no-longer unfurrowed brow. The bleak, sharp features of his face and a newly-acquired glittering in his eyes told me that his being, physical or mental, concealed an underground fire which hardly any longer was to be quenched.

When, besides, from repeated attacks of coughing, I then believed I understood that his leaning forward towards me could just as easily have its basis in that he was tired and sought to rest against the edge of the table, as in the interest of the conversation, I decided on the spot to enter right into the question of the state of his health and thus to put myself in the possession of another important outwork of his confidence.

I suddenly rose, determined and sombre, and said that I, as an experienced physician, unfortunately saw that he was rather more ill than he himself possibly thought, and that since he was clearly weakened and faint — I cited the drops of sweat on his brow — at least he should right away sit himself here on the comfortable sofa, which I had taken up so far.

He acknowledged that he had not coped well with climbing the stairs those two times — the first time he had only gone down to put an end to that nasty draught through the building — and willingly sat according to my wish on the sofa.

It was his chest, he said. With the aid of my stethoscope and by percussing with my fingers I discovered, unfortunately, that he was all too right.

It was his chest, but in such a condition that it was only a matter of winning time, not of healing; for one lung was completely gone and the other seriously affected.

In the latter part of the evening both he and I felt that we had been reborn on our old footing. Besides, my authority as a physician gave me ever so slightly the upper hand.

At nine o'clock I explained that he must go to bed, and told him that I intended to come again the following forenoon and prescribe the necessaries for him. He had to teach, I heard, at the alms-school, from eleven o'clock that day — until that time he promised not to go out. —

— When I came home, I found my wife very anxious about me.

She could not grasp that a sensible man and moreover a doctor, who gave others such careful advice, could go about more than was necessary in such weather; and I had after all been out in it the whole time, nearly since noon.

To this there was nothing to say, and I simply meditated whilst she spoke, upon how best I should win her assent to the matter which I now had at heart.

My wife was not in any way acquainted with my mortally-ill friend, and she might even, if I knew her right, turn out to be hurt when I told her that he had in a way owned my youth's affections before her.

And it turned out quite as I had predicted. It was only after a rather disturbingly long pause that she suddenly came over and said that my best friend would naturally also be very dear to her.

Nor from that moment could anyone have been more zealous than she.

For in whatever she sets out to do she always does it thoroughly, and that very evening she settled how the matter should be arranged.

At ten o'clock the following forenoon my wife and I were up with my friend, and I introduced her to him, saying that she wished to be regarded as a friend of his of equally long standing, as was I.

I told him, as cheerfully as I could — but as I said it my wife looked away — that his illness absolutely required that he stay indoors on a cure for six months, until the warm summer came and could complete his recovery, and also that I hoped he would consent to my settling matters with the alms-school for him.

He was evidently both surprised and moved.

Life had not offered him friendship, he said; he was so little used to accepting it, even when it was as true and good as here.

After some parleying, however, he finally gave in unconditionally to my wife, who does not like to lose.

He did not wish meanwhile to move into our house, as I proposed, since he had grown fond of this room and — as he openly said — he would not feel happy about bringing economic obligations, which he moreover did not need, into the matter.

From now on I visited him as a rule every forenoon, and would also usually strike up a little chat then about various things out in town, which I imagined might interest or at least divert him.

My wife took matters up in her own way.

Contrary to what I had been a mite afraid of, she did not carry out any thoroughgoing revolution in his housekeeping or wonted arrangements. That the housemaid had her grounds for seeing up to him so often, and that she daily, trembling, awaited my wife's silent inspection of whether the dust was gone and the room in order — of these things he could have had no inkling. All that my wife openly initiated was all sorts of supplies of fortifying things. The maid who took these would often be accompanied by one of our children, and he would sometimes find pleasure in keeping them with him for a while and chatting with them.

This new, and for him unaccustomed situation did seem to divert him; but after the passage of a month his mood again began to become depressed. Our visits evidently burdened him, for which reason these were stopped for a while too. He would spend virtually the whole day on the sofa, over in the dark part of the room.

One evening, the maid related, she heard a kind of crying and sobbing inside his room; therefore she had not gone in but had remained standing outside. A little later it seemed to her it was as if he were praying so fervently, but she did not understand the words. The following evening she heard him playing a soft melody, as if on a violin, which sounded muted.

The following forenoon, when I went to him, his state of mind was quite changed, and to my surprise I realised that his violin hung polished and strung, although admittedly with the split in its front, upon the wall, with the bow at its side. Over on the table by the bed I noticed too an old Bible, which I had never seen before in his room; presumably because this treasure had always been kept safe in his chest of drawers as something sacred.

He looked more than usually frail and worn out, but his face wore a transfigured expression, as that of a man who has struggled with his fate and now won rest and resignation.

If it were possible, he said, he would like to talk to my wife that same forenoon, but to me he wished rather to talk right away, and I should therefore sit a while with him.

With a smile — that same, still smile of his own beautiful secret, which I knew so well from the old days, but which somehow no longer needed to avoid attention now — he turned to me and said, as he laid his hand upon my shoulder and looked me in the eyes:

'My dear, kindhearted Frederick! I cannot tell you why, but I know for certain that I shall not live so long as to see spring again. What I need, neither you nor any person can give me, only Our Lord; but of all people you've been closest to me, and your friendship has reached deeper than you could have imagined. You have a right to know the person who has been your friend. When I'm gone — and that will occur without fail this winter, perhaps sooner than you, judging by the state of my illness, might think — then you'll find a number of notes in my drawer. They are the story of my earliest youth, but, simple as it is, it has for me decided my whole life. It will tell you that the world has been burdensome for me, sorely burdensome, and that I was as happy as a freed bird to leave it.

'There was a time,' he added after some hesitation, 'when I most wished to be buried by a church up in Nordland; now I think, however, that the place itself does not matter, and that one can rest just as peacefully down here.'

With this he squeezed my hand and bade me send my wife to

15

him.

When she came she was surprised to see him so bright and easy of mind, which she had never imagined that he could be.

He wished, he said, to request a favour of her friendship. It was a caprice of his; but if he should be called away, she must promise him the following spring to plant a wild rose on his grave.

How sorrowful his request was, my wife understood only when I had told her what had passed before; for David Holst himself had appeared so unafraid and bright when he spoke to her that the sorrow had, as it were, been forgotten. My friend's prophecy about himself unfortunately proved to be all too true. Although his mood steadily became brighter, so that sometimes a ray of *joie de vivre* would even shine in him, his illness always went the opposite way, however, to the worse.

One day I found him out of his bed — where he now for the most part spent the whole day — very interestedly lying and examining how my little Anton had made a 'steamship' out of his old violin-case, whose cover was missing, and with which he was now calling at all sorts of foreign ports on the floor. When I came over to the bed he said, smiling, that he had been home in Nordland and played on the shore again.

My wife had more and more become his nurse now. She would be with him a couple of times a day and sit at his bedside. He liked to hold her hand then, or he would also ask her to read something to him from his old Bible. The subjects he chose were especially those in which the Old Testament tells of love between lovers. In particular he dwelled on the story of Jacob and Rachel.

My wife, who had by now grown sincerely fond of him, confided in me one day that she indeed thought she knew what my friend suffered from; it was surely nothing else but unhappy love.

So movingly beautiful, as he lay there approaching death, she had never imagined that a person could be.

When he lay still and smiled it was as if he were thinking about a tryst to which he would go as soon as he was finished with us here on Earth.

One evening he asked my wife to sit with him.

At nine o'clock I was called; but when I arrived he was no more.

For the first time he had asked my wife to read a part of the *Song of Solomon* to him, where she found an old mark in his Bible. It was the second chapter, in which both the bride and the bridegroom speak, and which begins thus:

I am the rose of Sharon, and the lily of the valleys

and ends with:

Until the day break, and the shadows flee away,
turn, my beloved, and be thou like a roe or young hart
upon the mountains of Bether.

He had asked her to read it twice, but during the reading he had quietly fallen asleep.

And there he lay wonderful in death, with a quiet smile, as if he were now greeting just such a grove on the other side, in the mountains of Bether.

The next summer a wooden cross and a flowering wild dog-rose stood on a grave out in the town churchyard.

There rests my friend David Holst.

I found, placed as a beginning to my friend's life story, a section of which a part seems to have been added at a more mature age. It shows with what strong ties he has been bound by nature to his home, and with what love he has clung to it.

David Holst's Notes
Nordland and the Nordlander

Insofar as a person such as I, who lives in such a sorrowful reality, dares to speak of illusions — what numbers of and what great illusions have I had not crushed then, here in Kristiania, in the two to three years since I left my home in Nordland and became a student — how grey and dull is not this world down

17

here, how petty and niggardly compared to what I had imagined to myself both the people and conditions!

I was out fishing in the fjord with some friends this afternoon, and naturally we all enjoyed ourselves — except me, who however gave an excellent appearance of doing so.

No, I did not enjoy myself!

We sat in a flat-bottomed, broad, ugly boat they called the 'Punt', a contrivance that resembles a wash-tub, and all afternoon in muddy water at a depth of a few feet, with a thin line we caught altogether no fewer than 7, seven whiting — and then one rowed contented back to land!

I felt nearly nauseous: for, like this punt without a keel by which it could set a course, without a sail, which could not even be thought properly to be fitted to it, without a sea swell, which it would not tolerate, and like this muddy, grey, waveless sea outside the town with some few whiting in it — seems to me life as a whole down here. It has in no respect anything else to offer but small whiting like those.

Whilst the others talked I sat and thought about a fishing trip when *she* was there, out between the Sprite Skerries at home, in our little six-oared boat. What a different day, what a different boat, what a different adventure!

Yes, how adventureless, poor and grey life is down here on the rich, corn-bearing, clayey slopes and on the capital's fjord, sooty from steamship smoke, or here in the town itself, compared to at home.

But had I hinted this aloud, these haughty folk would surely have stared in wonder.

They speak of fishing here and mean thereby some miserable hauls of cod and whiting.

A Nordlander understands thereby, as in everything else, the thousandfold: he means the millions caught off the Lofotens and Finmark, and, besides, an overflowing multiplicity of species from the whales that blow in the sounds, with great, cascading schools of fish before them, down to the very smallest.

The only noteworthy fish I know of down here, and which I always look at whenever I find one, is the goldfish, which one keeps in a bowl just as one keeps a canary in a cage; but that again is from another fairytale land in the South.

Nor by bird does a Nordlander picture to himself, as down

here, just some wildfowl or other, but a whole sky-full of all sorts, surging in the air like a white surf around the nesting cliffs, a whole screeching, teeming blizzard above the egg-sites.

He is reminded of the eider duck, the black guillemot, the duck and the oyster-catcher swimming in the fjord and sound, or sitting around on the skerries; of the seagulls, the fish-hawk and osprey hunting in the air, of the great horned owl hooting horribly at night from out in the mountain clefts — in short, he means a whole world of birds, and it pains him somewhat to restrict the term to just some poor, pitiful capercaillie or other, which one is heartless enough to surprise and kill in the middle of its courtship, whilst the sun rises, up on a hillside of fir trees.

Instead of the berry fields here he has the miles and miles of cloudberry bogs at home. —

Instead of the beach down here, rather monotonously lacking in seashells, he remembers one which is strewn with the most wonderfully coloured multiplicity of them.

Nordland has without doubt all natural conditions to an intensive degree and in quite otherwise, enormously mighty contrasts.

It has an endless stone grey wilderness as in the beginning of time, before people settled, but in the midst of this too its endless profusions of nature. It has sun and a summer glory whose day is not just twelve hours long, but lasts uninterrupted, day and night for three months, when in many places one has to wear a mask because of the midge swarms. — But by contrast again, a night of darkness and terror which lasts for nine.

These are giant conditions, but without the more undistinguished transitions midway between all extremes, upon which the calm life here in the South is built; they are in other words conditions more for imagination, adventure and risk than for level-headed reason and quiet, steady work.

A Norlander can therefore, to begin with, down here easily feel like a Gulliver who has come to Lilliput, and who hardly fits in at all amongst the inhabitants until he has had his accustomed conceptions screwed down to the prosaic dimensions of this lesser reality: in short, until he learns to use reason instead of imagination.

The Lapp on his skis with his reindeer, the Kvæn, the Russian, not to mention the Nordlander himself, steadily travelling, slow on land but rapid in his boat — are indisputably all much more interesting folk than the grey oats-farmer, whose imagination

19

hardly stretches further from his own fields than to wondering where on earth, up in the outlying fields, the nag might be found now.

When they speak of storms and waves then they mean here a bit of storm and sea swell in Kristiania fjord, which might even bring about a little 'damage in the harbour', and find it so exceedingly shocking when a clumsy boatman is lost at sea.

Something quite different comes into my thoughts then: sudden squalls from the mountains, which take away houses — which is why one has to lash them down with ropes at home — waves, in from the Arctic Sea, which bury the high skerries and holms in spray and which 'touch bottom' in many fathoms' depth of water, so that a vessel suddenly comes to stand on the dry bed and is crushed in the middle of the sea. —

Bands of brave men who sail before the weather for their lives — and not just for their own lives, but with a dearly-won cargo for their kin too, who are sitting at home — and who even in the midst of mortal danger try to give their capsized comrade a helping hand. — I think of the loss of numerous boats and vessels on winter evenings in the driving scud and on the waves — indeed, it could for once be worth seeing them (normally three in succession and the last wave the worst) on the approach: with combs of spray higher than the custom-house roofs and perhaps a sloop, which has to be put in to land, on their shoulders, sweeping into Kristiania's peaceful, narrow harbour, hurling ships up into the town, and followed by correspondingly heavy storm gusts, so that the roofs were lifted off. —

I know well that if they came it is me they would fetch, that poor 'seer' concealed in the civilisation of the town, who, they think, belongs to them. But I would perhaps, even so, for a moment in my mortal dread have greeted them as friends from home, even although they came with bodies and wrecks on their shoulders.

They would for once show all the civilised pettifogging in here the mighty sea's terror and greatness, and cast a pinch of pungent mortal dread into all this insipidity.

I should like to have seen a whale, squeezed between Prince and Tolbooth Streets, staring into a family on the topmost floor, or a battered sea draug whom the neat, gold-braided constables were trying to put into jail.

I should also like to have seen the town's petty theatre critics, who are used, twice a week, to seeing a *Haupt- und Staatsaction* in the vaudeville theatres, standing with their pince-nez on their noses before a performance like that, which without further ado would overflow all of their critical terms and inkwells and show them death and terror in full, crushing seriousness.

How much would not such a reviewer grow in his capacity to understand what is imposing and mighty in a composition and in desire thereafter, if he only once in his life had seen the 'Horseman' on a stormy day, his seventeen-hundred-foot-high ride southward out in the foaming sea, whilst his cape flits northward about his shoulder, and one sees as in a pure illusion, before the giant himself, in his might, the horse's head, ear, throat, the bit, and its majestic breast.

There, in the North, quite since the times of myth, folk conceptions have laid the home to all legions of evil.

There the Lapps have practised their magic crafts, cast spells, and there, by the dark, winter-grey, wave-troubled Arctic Sea the gods of old, driven to the furthest reaches of the earth, still seem to stand, the demonic, horrible, half-formed powers of darkness which the Æsir battled with but which first St Olaf, with his victorious, dazzling white cross-hilt properly had 'turned to stone'.

On the whole, what one so easily, sitting high and dry in the middle of civilisation, shuns as superstition — but which, however, still lives as a natural force in people — presents itself to the imagination on a quite different, puppet-like scale to people here in the South.

One has a little fright of small pixies, good-natured siren-folk, a love-sick water-sprite and so on, which in the North, with us, virtually go between the houses like superstition's tame, common pets.

One also has there good-natured 'underground folk', who peacefully use their boats and *jægts*, invisible beside the population.

But then nature's horror creates, besides, a whole legion of evil demons that compel people, drowned men's ghosts that miss Christian soil, mountain giants, the sea draug, who rows in a half-boat and screams horribly out in the fjord in the winter night. Many people, who really were in need, for fear of him have had to do without their livelihoods, and the 'seers' can see him.

But if nature's predominance broods like an oppressive weight over life on this winter-dark, sea-foaming boundary coast which shimmers faintly for nine months and for three of them even loses the sun, so that a terror of darkness is created in the mind — then Nordland also has to the same extremity the exact opposite characteristic: its warm, sunny, clear-aired, fragrance-filled summer nature whose beauty shifts in an endless wealth of colours, and in which distances of three- to four-score miles across the mirror of the sea close up to one another to shouting reach, in which the mountains clothe themselves in brown-green grass right to the top — in the Lofotens up to two thousand feet — in which forests of small birches wreathe upwards on wooded slopes and mountain ravines like a frolic of white, sixteen-year-old girls, whilst the flavour of strawberry and raspberry, which grow there, can be sensed in the air as nowhere else as you come past, in shirtsleeves because of the heat, and the day is so hot that you feel the need to bathe in the sun-filled, rippling sea, strangely clear right to the bottom.

That all vegetation acquires such a strong flavour and colour up there the learned have explained by the strong light that fills the air, since the sun is up around the clock, without a break. Neither, therefore, *can* any such tasty strawberries or raspberries or such fragrant birch twigs be found anywhere else as there.

Has a wondrously delightful idyll any home, then it must be in Nordland's fjord valleys in the summer.

It is as if the sun then kisses nature so much more fervently for the sake of the short time that it knows they have together, and as if they both for the while seek to forget that they so soon must part again. Then the grass and wild flowers burst out as if by some sudden wonder and in a profuse multiplicity of bluebells, dandelions, buttercups, oxeye daisies, dog roses, raspberries and strawberries by every burn, about every hillock, on every wooded hillside; then hundreds of black insects hum in the grass as if in a tropical country; then cows, horses and sheep are driven up the valleys and onto the mountainsides, whilst the Lapp from the highlands comes down to the fjord valley with his reindeer and waters them at the river; then the cloudberry bogs lie blushing for miles inland; then there is peace and sunshine and quiet in every hut, where the fisherman now sits, at home with his own, mending his tackle for the winter fishings; then there is in Nordland a summer as beautiful as only a few other places know, and an idyllic peace and joy of nature as perhaps nowhere else.

From this caressing softness of nature too, the Nordlander acquires a trait in his character: he is fond, when he can afford to, of living and dressing well and dwelling comfortably; with regard to delicacies he is a real epicure. Cod tongues, young ptarmigan, reindeer marrow, salted rose fish, trout, salmon, and all sorts of saltwater fish of the best quality, served with their trimmings of liver and roe, the nourishing reindeer meat and all kinds of game are, together with the fresh-tasting cloudberries, just ordinary dishes for him.

The Lapp as well as the common Nordlander enjoys, besides, even as a child all sorts of sweet relishes, and the 'syrup on his porridge' is widely known.

Brought up in a nature so rich in contrasts and possibilities, and on the unexpected in the whole repertoire of nuances from the most widely grand to the tearfully intense, lovely and enchanting, the Nordlander has, as a rule, a good and quick, often brilliant and imaginative mind.

Impressionable as he is, he gives himself up to the moment. If there is sunshine in your face, there will most likely be sunshine in his, too.

But one should not mistake him and confuse his good-naturedness with simple confidence — and people here in the South do that often. Inside his soul the quiet suspicion sways, unknown to him, always, like a vigilant sea-bird, which ducks under whilst the priming is still flashing and before the bullet has had time to hit the place in the sea where the bird has just been.

The sudden, the possibility of anything and everything, he has since his childhood out in nature been used to imagining as a sword, hanging over every peaceful, quiet moment, and he usually carries that instinct with him in his relations with people.

Whilst you are speaking to him he might duck under into his soul like that, and do so time and again without your having an inkling of it, and without the mood being interrupted.

He does this whilst he has tears in his eyes at the most sincerely touching moment — it is but his nature, of which he will always retain a trace, even after he has moved with all of his family from his life in nature into civilised circumstances. He avoids you, slips with his imagination and wary suspicion in between and around your thoughts: indeed, were he a truly gifted Nordlander — I am too feeble and uninterested to be able to do this — I believe that, without your knowing it, he could walk right through your soul with his hands in his pockets, in by the brow and out by the back of your head.

As a detective or diplomat he would be inestimable, if he had only had more character and laid less childishly weak in the face of the power of the moment: but here, unfortunately, is his weak side.

I speak here of that deep trait in a people's character, insofar as it is revealed in the more prominent types, and do not wish to be misunderstood as if I meant that there should not also be found men of character in Nordland — there they are often, probably more than elsewhere, tempered to greatness.

In an indigenous Nordland stock there will most usually be found — at least this is my belief — some drops of Lappish blood.

It is also noted elsewhere that, when the sagas mention, of the best peasant families in Helgeland, that they are descended from half-trolls or mountain giants, this just indicates Lappish parentage. Our loyal lineages have Lappish origins, and Fin was a fitting name, carried by the best men in the land, for example Fin Arnesen.

Harald Fairhair and Eric Bloodaxe married Lappish girls.

The mystical, sensuously compelling might which has been ascribed them was only the erotic expression of a great national link through the ages between these two different racial elements: the light-haired, blue-eyed, mentally greater and calmer Norwegian and the dark, brown-eyed, quick-witted, fanciful Lapp, filled with a mysticism about nature but weak in character and oppressed, whose prototype to this day stands on his skis and sings melancholy chants inside the mind of many a Norwegian, who in his racial chauvinism little suspects that he has ties with that people.

In addition, in my experience, a great difference in character manifests itself depending on whether the blending was with the weak Lapp or with the well-built, strong, persevering Finn: the Kvæn. It makes for a difference in temperament as between major and minor in one and the same *Phantasiestück*.

The blending with Lapps has been a major and important factor in the constitution of the present Norwegian people's mental characteristics.

The blending with Kvæns gives energetic, logical, persevering people who are keen traders; it has certainly to a great extent put the steel into the characters of our peoples from Østland and Trondhjem. In Nordland, on the contrary, the blending with Lapps has been predominant and has to some extent changed the character of the people up there. The Kvæn-Norwegian is victorious over nature in Nordland; the Lapp-Norwegian lies more underneath it and suffers under its weight.

The contrasts in the nature of Nordland are too strong and extreme for the minds of those who live up there not to be highly vulnerable to being cracked by it.

The great brooding and sadness which is found there, in the ordinary man too, and which so often results in mental derangement and suicide, surely has a profound relationship with and basis in these natural surroundings, in the long winter darkness with its heavy, overwhelming scenes which crush the mind down in lonely absence of light, and in the strong and sudden impressions which equally in the dark as in the light times all too violently seize at the innermost, fine strings of the temperament.

I have thought over these things as hardly anyone else, thought, whilst I myself have suffered from them, and I understand — although when it concerns my own person, again I do not understand at all — why 'second sight', 'the other sight', 'seeing' as it is called in Nordland, there as on the Shetland and Orkney Islands can come about and be passed down in the family. I understand that it is an ailment of the soul, which no cure, no reason or reflection can cure.

One is born with a third window in the house of one's soul besides one's two healthy eyes, a window that looks out to a world which others only have an inkling of, but that one oneself is condemned, when the compulsion comes, to having to go across to and look out of: it does not let itself be stopped up with books or by any reasonable reflection, nor be walled up even here in the middle of the 'enlightened capital', at most just dimmed a while by the curtain of forgetfulness.

Oh, when I recall how I went about at home in Nordland and pictured to myself the King's castle in Kristiania, with its pinnacles and towers projecting grandly over the capital, and the King's men like a golden stream from the court right up to the throne room, or the Akershus fortress when the cannons, thundering, announced the King's arrival, whilst the air as in a storm was filled with martial music and mighty royal commands. — When I think, how

I pictured to myself the 'High Hall of Light', the University, as a great, white, chalk edifice, always with sunshine in the window-panes, or how I portrayed for myself the Storting chamber and the men who went about there, and whose names, magnified by the imagination, carried up to us as if for each a mighty, ringing bell pealed in the air. —

When I compare what I pictured to myself in Nordland with all this, with the 'respectable enough reality for our limited circumstances' in which I now live and circulate — then it is as if a house of cards of illusions, as high as Snehætten, collapses over me.

I have indeed, until I was some years over twenty, lived only in a Nordland fairy tale, and am really now, for the first time, born into the real world; I have been spell-bound in my own imagination.

Were I to tell anyone all this, he would — and the more rational the man was, the more surely this would happen — certainly discover that my excellent *Examen Artium* must surely have come about through an obvious mistake. Where, in the meantime, theoretical *raisonnement* and knowledge are concerned, there I have skills just as good as anyone's, thank God. I know too, that in them I have that pair of pliant oars with which, as far as I require, I shall be able to row my boat through the practical life without running aground.

The load which I have in the boat, so burdensome, so burden-some, and at its times so blissfully delightful too, no-one may see.

I feel a deep need to weep away my whole Nordland fairy tale and would do that, if I could only thereby weep my life away too. But why wish to lose all that is delightful, the whole illusion, when I shall anyway have to carry to the hour of my death the burden that it has laid upon me!

My easing weeping will be, in quiet hours, to paint my life's memories from this my home, which so few down here understand.

It is a poor, soul-sick man's tale, in which there are to be found more of his own impressions than outside events.

Chapter 1
Home

My father was a local trader, and owned the trading post . . . ven in the West Lofotens.

He was actually from Trondhjem, whence he had come north as a boy without means, with a trading ship of the kind which usually is sent from there to Lofoten to trade during the fishings.

In his youth he had had to go through a great deal, and for a time even had to work in a boat crew as a common fisherman, until he eventually came to work as store-boy for the trader Erlandsen, whose son-in-law he became.

My father was, when middle-aged, a handsome man, black-haired, swarthy, with sharp, energetic facial features and short rather than tall. He always wore a brown duffle seaman's jacket and a white oil-cloth hat. In bearing he was harsh and not very approachable; it was said, too, that he was rather a hard man — something in which the strict school of life that he had gone through was possibly to blame.

If his bearing earned him but few personal friends, then it did on the other hand obtain him so much the greater authority in his business, in which he was prompt and efficient, although obstinate to the extreme about what he believed to be his right. People feared him and would reluctantly be on bad terms with him.

Of what one experiences before one's eighth year one usually only has a glimpsed memory, but in return these glimpses last for all of one's life.

And of my poor, unhappy mother I carry in my soul such a picture. I know her from that better than from everything that I was later to hear of her, and according to which she had, amongst other things, light-coloured hair and kind, blue eyes, had a weak chest and was pale, in stature quite tall. She was apparently also

27

very quiet and very sad in her ways.

She was Erlandsen's only daughter, and was married to my father whilst he was still an underling in Erlandsen's employ, and it was said that it was old Erlandsen who had brought about this union, as he believed thereby best to secure her future.

It was a warm summer's day. The mowers stood in shirtsleeves and swung their scythes, out in the meadow. I accompanied my mother, who walked past them, knitting.

Above the fence lay a half-bare rock, behind which my mother had a bench. Above that, in a pile of stones there grew raspberry bushes, and beside it stood several low birches.

Whilst I was crawling about in between the stones and tasting the raspberries, father called my mother.

When she had gone away, there came from the other side across to me a tall, pale lady, who looked older than my mother, clothed in black, with a stiff, white, piped ruff. She looked at me in such a friendly way, and seemingly proffered me a wild dog-rose, which she had in her hand.

I was not at all frightened, nor was it as if she were a stranger. Then she nodded mournfully to me, as a parting, and walked away the same way that she had come.

When my mother came back, I told her that there had been such a nice, strange lady, but that she was surely very grieved, and now she was gone.

My mother — I remember it as if it were a moment ago — stood still a while, white as a sheet, looking at me with fear in her eyes, as if the pair of us were both to die now, then she threw her arms together over her head and fell down in a faint.

I was too frightened to scream, but I think I remember that whilst she lay there, stretched lifeless on the grass above the bench, I threw myself over and cried: 'Mother!'

A little later I had come running across to father, who was standing in his shirtsleeves over on the meadow and was cutting hay with the others, and had said, sobbing, that mother was dead now.

From that moment on my mother was mentally deranged.

She had to be watched over in her own room for many years, and my father surely had many a difficult hour.

Later she was taken to a mental asylum in Trondhjem, where she died two years afterwards without having come to her senses for an instant.

The person who looked after me during that time was old Anna Kvæn, a pock-marked, masculine woman with small, brown eyes, wiry steel-grey hair and nearly witch-like marked features, usually also with a short, black, clay pipe in her mouth.

She had been my mother's nanny and stood by her with all of her soul. After my mother became mentally ill, she had keenly asked to 'keep watch' in the blue room; but this had to be given up when it became clear that precisely her presence most excited the patient's mind. Nor could my mother bear to see father, and they did not even dare show her me.

Old Anna Kvæn had been my mother's only confidant in this life. She was extremely superstitious and peculiar in her ways. To her powers of suggestion the pixie and the draug were just as surely there, down in the sea-shed and in the boat-house as my father resided in the main building, and underneath the mountain on the eastern side of the harbour the 'underground folk' carried on their fishing and sailed their sloops to Bergen invisibly, just as my father did these things visibly at the base of it.

She had surely filled up my poor mother's head with her mystical superstition to no less a degree than she filled mine. There were all kinds of marks and signs to consider from morning to evening, and she always wore an uneasy expression, as if she were keeping watch. When a boat came, one had to turn towards the sea and spit and mumble some words against the sea-sprites. She saw every man's fetch and spectre. Because of these the door should not be closed too hastily after someone who has gone out, and she could always hear a warning in advance when father came home from a journey.

When Anna Kvæn was no longer allowed to go into the blue room to mother, in silence she would perform a whole host of tricks outside the door. I remember thus, that I once stood on the stair and saw her bowing, curtseying and intermittently drawing with spittle on the door and mumbling, until I ran away in dread.

In her incantations the name 'Jumala' often occurred, the name of the old god of the *Bjarmer* which up there in the far North is rather less eradicated than one might think, and which even to this day, perhaps, still has one or two sacrificial stones out in the mountain plateau in Finmark. Against 'Lappish spells' she had her preventative measures too. She obviously blended the Kvæn and the Christian gods in her mystical incantations in order to conquer the Lappish magic.

Under these influences on my mind I grew up.

The manse, with the white, steepled church beside it, lay only a short way from us, down by the sea at the right-hand side of the bay, when one looked out from our trading post, which lay innermost in it.

There they had a tutor — we always called him the 'Student'.

I went to school there every day with the minister's two children, a bright boy by the name of Carl, who was one year younger than I, that is, twelve, and his sister Susanna — exactly the same age as I — a blue-eyed, unruly child with a mass of golden hair which had always to be flicked from her brow, and who, when she could get away with it unnoticed by the Student, would steadily make all kinds of faces and grimaces across to us two others in order to make us laugh.

The tutor was indeed sorely strict and inspired extreme respect. The urge to laugh, which on such occasions we sat in torment from, not daring to look up at each other so that it might not come to expression, was actually anything but funny, for every time we exploded we all suffered sorely, in that as a first act there was a boxing of ears, and thereafter long, written harangues in our report books about our conduct.

Susanna was often perfectly merciless in this. It had indeed reached the point where with just a little wink in the corner of one eye she could spark off the whole feverish condition in us, so that we sat flushed red in the cheeks like apples with our stiff, staring gazes nailed to our books, until it held no longer. Especially she affected me, who she well knew had to pay for it heavily at home; for father was a hard man who understood children all too little.

In our free time we played as wildly as surely few children have played.

Compared to the strict and dark life at home, where father was busy either out in his shop or up in his office, where from the blue room there could now and again be heard noises and shouts from my poor, demented mother, and where Anna Kvæn always roamed about almost like an unpleasant spirit, playing with the children of the manse was like a life over on a different joyful, sunny side of the world.

Chapter 2
On the Shore

Even more than here in the South of Norway, the shore in Nordland is a compelling place for children to play. During low tide the sea-bed lies dry far out, quite differently than here in the South.

The clay-like surface of the sand lies bare then, with occasional pools in it where young fish swim, whilst on the outermost edge, out by the sea, walks a wader or two, or a lonesome seagull sits on a rock. The wave-patterned, fine, sandy clay is full of hummocks covered in whorls left by the large, sought-after worm which wriggles into the ground there. Hidden amongst the stones or amongst the seaweed lie the small, swift, clear-as-glass, shrimp-like 'sandhoppers', which, when they are pursued, dart through the shallow water. They are used by little boys as bait, on fish-hooks made of pins, for catching young coalfish.

On the high, grassy bank above the beach, between some large stones, we three children built our own trading place from flat stone slabs, with a sea-shed, boat-house and jetty underneath.

In the boat-house we had all sorts of boats, large and small, from the four-oared rowing boat right up to the five-boarder, partly made from wood and bark, partly from the boat-shaped blue mussel shells. Our pride and joy, the big *jægt* — a large, repaired, trough with one mast and a 'loose deck', which was constantly being equipped for the 'Bergen gathering' — was not the best, however. I still recall how many a time I would sit in the church and imagine the fairy tale of our owning that glorious, fully-rigged ship with the cannons, which hung up there beneath the chancel arch, and how, whilst the minister was preaching, I would fantasise about all kinds of voyages, which Carl, but especially Susanna, would have been sorely amazed to have seen. That ship was the

31

only thing that I then lacked in my happiness.

Inwith the bay, by father's jetty, there was a deep 'shelving' in the sea, where in the late summer schools of roach and other small fish swam, and where we boys went fishing, each with his flaxen line with a pin hook on the end. We would cut the fish up, hang it, split, over the branches of the drying racks we had erected across the ground over by our own trading place, and would prepare it as dried fish, whilst we let the liver stand across in small vessels and rot until it turned into oil. Both products were then correctly stacked over in our sea-shed, later to 'go to Bergen' on the *jægt*, and, God knows, we were occupied, worked and slaved just as keenly and seriously at our task as the adults did at theirs, although our only real reward was just the sunshine that we got across our browned faces.

Carl was a slightly-built boy who on the whole followed his more energetic sister in everything. Both of the children of the manse had thick, golden hair. Susanna's coiled up, lock by lock, so that it almost sparkled around her head whenever she moved — something which, as mentioned earlier, she constantly did with a toss to keep it from her brow. Both of them had in addition very white and pure skin and had delightful blue eyes. I am not sure whether Susanna was then tall or short for her age — in any case I imagined her to be at least as tall as I, although she must certainly have been at least half a head shorter; the rest of the measure surely being made up by my admiration.

I recall how she would go to church on Sundays together with her mother — a small, pale, darkly-dressed, hard-working woman who always, except on Sunday forenoon, was knitting at a long, sad stocking. She would walk along the sand-strewn road to the church finely dressed, wearing a white or blue dress and with a dark shepherdess' hat on her head, a little white kerchief folded together behind a very big, old hymn book, and white stockings and on her feet shoes with bands crossed over the instep. A prettier attire than Susanna's Sunday best I did not believe could be found in the whole world.

In church, the minister's family sat in the first pew, directly under the pulpit, and we — my father and I — sat a couple of rows behind, and we would exchange then many a freemason's sign, intelligible only to us.

Once, though, Susanna hurt me deeply — indeed to bitter

tears. For it became clear to me that she had made even my father into the target of her merry observations.

With his good, strong voice he sang the hymns in the naïve way of country folk, very loudly, but added — something which at the time I and many others found very engaging — to the end of each verse a personal flourish that did not belong to the tune, but was of his own composition. This had been the occasion for talk in the manse, and Susanna's little pitcher had had big ears then too. When she noticed that I had discovered this, she looked sorely unhappy.

When Carl was thirteen years old he was sent to grammar school in Bergen, and the 'costly' tutor left with the last steamship the same autumn.

Susanna received her education from her parents from now on, and I had to take my learning with the sacristan, a good-natured old man who himself knew little apart from how to play the violin, which he did with a passion, and admittedly too with an, albeit disorderly, talent of genius.

Since the sacristan had obtained permission from my father for me to learn to play, and I, just as the sacristan, thought better of this preoccupation than of my lessons, three whole years passed, or the time until beyond my sixteenth year, divided in a way between playing the violin and idleness.

Had my spirit in that period of my life been held suitably under the daily discipline of labour, much about me would perhaps later have turned out differently. As it was, I was forsaken to all of my imaginings in a violence, and had rooted in me moods which later, to a pernicious degree, became the masters of my life.

That dividing line which is drawn in everyone's consciousness between imagination and reality, certain natures, who live under a strong impressionability, need to have sternly and repeatedly demarcated, otherwise it is easily erased at certain points and goes over into illness.

Regardless that we now no longer had the same abundant opportunity as before to come together, Susanna and I were nonetheless throughout our adolescence constant playfellows and confidants.

When she had something to confide in me, she would usually wait by the gate that crossed the road over by the manse grounds, at the times when I used to walk to or from the sacristan's.

One day, as I came walking along the road home with my books under my arm she was sitting, in her blue chequered blouse and shepherdess' hat, on the stile beside the gate. She appeared to be in a very bad mood, and I realised right away that something was coming.

She did not reply to my greeting; but when, more hastily than she thought proper, I sought to slip through the gate, she asked me in a heated tone if it were true, as they said, that I was so lazy that nothing would become of me at home.

Susanna had often teased me; but what annoyed me this time was that I realised that in the manse they had been critical of my family, and that Susanna had participated in it.

Had I known that Susanna sat there that day as my defeated supporter I would certainly have treated matters differently than I did, for now I walked off with a hurt expression, without deigning her a word.

When I came home I heard that the minister and my father had disagreed in the Arbitrating Commission. The minister, who was the Commissioner, had expressed that he thought my father had acted too harshly in some matter, and my father had given him an abrupt answer. It was in this connection that the criticism of us had now spilled out at the manse.

This relationship between the adults gave an insecure shyness to us children, and I recall that to begin with I was even afraid to go past the manse, since I might possibly meet the minister on the way.

Susanna meanwhile made various attempts at reconciliation, but at the slightest glimpse of her blue chequered dress I always took long detours over the fields above the road, or would wait in amongst the trees until she was gone.

For a few days I saw nothing of her; but as I passed through the gate one day, I saw, written in pencil on the white sign of the district boundary post:

You are cross with me, but S. is not at all cross with you.

That big, clumsy handwriting I knew well enough, and I turned back to the gate two or three times that same day to read it again and again. This was Susanna in a new shape; I saw her in my thoughts behind the characters as if behind a railing.

That afternoon I added underneath:

Look behind the post!

And there I wrote:

D. is not cross with S. either.

The following day Susanna was standing in the garden by the trellis when I went past, but pretended that she did not see me; she probably regretted having been too quick to reconcile with me.

Although relations were outwardly polite to the highest degree, my father's dealings with the minister were from that time on basically broken off: they never, apart from at particular occasions and after solemn bidding, put a foot inside the other's door. This in its turn gave Susanna's and my meetings a certain surreptitious nature. Although there was no prohibition placed on us, somehow we nevertheless only met surreptitiously.

We were both lonesome children. Susanna sat trapped in everyday tedium at home under her mother's strict attention, and in my sad home I always felt that I was freezing and scared, and that all joy lay across in the manse, by Susanna. It was therefore no wonder that we always longed to see one another.

As we grew older the opportunities came less often, but the longing was thereby just bottled up in us, and those moments when we could be together gradually acquired — unknown to us — a different character to the old, child-like one. To talk with her had now become a solace for me, and many a day I would wander about by the manse just to catch a glimpse of her.

I was close upon sixteen years old when, one morning as I came past the garden of the manse, she waved me over and across the wall handed me a flower. She thereupon hastily ran in, right across the carrot beds, as if she were frightened that someone might see.

That was the first time that I realised that she was so pretty, and I thought of her for a long time, her standing there in the garden between the bushes with the morning sun upon her.

Chapter 3
The Servants' Quarters

The ghostly atmosphere which permeated our house was really properly aired only down in the servants' quarters, when the labourers and the maids and those common travellers who took overnight lodgings would sit by the red gleam from the iron stove of an evening and tell stories of all sorts of shipwrecks and ghostliness.

On the bench, in the space between the stove and the wall, sat the good-looking, strong Jens Prentice with his joinery and repair work around him; he was happy really just to do his work and listen to the others in silence.

By the stove 'Brogue Nils' was busy oiling brogues or leather garments — he had his name from his work, sewing brogues. Brogue Nils was a small fellow with an unruly yellow forelock that hung down over his brow, a face round as a moon, in which his nose sat like a little knob, and when he laughed his thin-lipped, wide mouth with those large jaws took on an expression rather like a dead man's grin. His small, milky eyes would squint secretively then, and said as well that he had a keen mind. Really it was he who knew most of the stories, but even more it was he who could persuade the strangers to tell stories, as the case might be: both from the seen and the unseen worlds.

A third lad had a nickname — which one did not use so that he could hear it, though — Anders Leadhat, so called because he would now and again have bad turns when he would drink and be on the verge of losing his job. But he was, in his way, extremely able. When in a real pinch — in a storm — he would at once step into the responsible position of being the headman in the boat; for of his superior ability on a sea journey there was but one opinion. When the danger was over he would again sink back to being his insignificant self.

To the fixed establishment of servants in the house there also belonged a girl, twenty years old, whom we called 'French Martine'. She was somehow of a quite different race than is usual in Nordland, was lively and bright, with very curly black hair around a brown, oval face with strikingly regular lines. She was slightly built and of medium height and good figure. Her eyes, under their heavy, black brows, were dark as coal; when she was exasperated they would simply spark.

She was in love with the silent Jens Prentice and without any grounds was extremely jealous. It was said that the two would make a match when he had finished with a couple more fishing trips, but the matter was not official, though, and as I believe it, it was because Jens Prentice passively resisted for as long as he could, and never expressly proposed.

French Martine was by origin one of those illegitimate children of the fishing districts up there whose fathers are foreign skippers or sailors. Her father was said to have been a French sailor.

To go into the servants' quarters of an evening was stricly forbidden to me by my father; he must have known that things were said there which were not for a child's ear.

But on the other hand, though, precisely down there were told the most interesting things that I could imagine in the world. The result was that I would secretly sneak down there.

I remember thus how one dark autumn evening, when I had stolen down there, I listened while Brogue Nils — the one with the yellow face and the dead man's grin when he laughed — told a horrible ghost story from the time of Erlandsen's predecessor.

At that time there stood an old sea-shed a short way outwith the manse.

And the story was that one Christmas Eve they sat drinking and celebrating inside the trading post. At eleven o'clock the beer ran out, and so the apprentice, who was called Rasmus and was a strong and brave chap, was sent across to the sea-shed where the beer barrel lay, to fill up a huge jug in a pewter mounting, which he had with him.

Across there Rasmus set the lamp on the barrel and began to draw. When the mug was filled, and he had just thought to put it to his lips, he saw, over the beer barrel, lying with its body in the dark where all the barrels stood row upon row, an awfully large, wide and dark shape which gave off an ice-cold breath, as from a door which was open. It blinked at him with a pair of huge eyes as if from a dim horn lantern and said:

'Thief in the Christmas beer.'

But Rasmus Prentice as not wanting. He hurled the heavy jug right into the draug's sight and then ran from the place with all his might.

Outside the moon was shining on the snow; he heard a screaming and hooting down on the shore, and sensed that draugs in greater and greater numbers were pursuing him.

When he came to the churchyard wall they were close to him, and then in his need to hit upon the expedient of calling in across it: 'Now help me, all the dead!' For the dead are enemies of the draugs.

Then he heard how they arose in there, and how there began a din and howling as if of a battle. Meanwhile he himself was resolutely pursued by a corpse, who was weighing him down just as he got hold of the door handle and slipped in, saved.

But there he fainted in the middle of the floor.

The following day — Christmas Day — the church-goers saw spread about over the graves pieces of coffin boards, and in between all kinds of old, waterlogged oars and boat planks of the sort which sink to the bottom after a shipwreck.

They were the weapons which the dead and the draugs had used, and from many things one could be sure that the dead had been the victors.

They also found, down in the sea-shed, both the pewter jug and the lamp. The pewter jug had been flattened against the draug's forehead, and the monster had crushed the lamp when the lad escaped.

Brogue Nils could also tell a great deal about 'seers' and their seeings, partly into the world of spirits, partly in reality itself, in which they either feel forebodings or — as by some kind of mirage for the inner sight — can see what is happening at that very moment at the furthest-away places.

They might sit in merry company and then all at once, pale and uneasy, stare absently into the air before them. What they see are manifold things, and then outcries sometimes escape them, such as: 'There's a fire in the buildings of trader N ... N ... in ... vaagen now', or: 'Trondhjem's burning now'.

Sometimes they see funeral processions passing, with such clarity that they can describe the position and appearance of every man in it, the coffin itself and the streets through which the procession is passing.

They might say then: 'A great man is being buried down in Kristiania now'.

When the news later comes it always agrees.

At sea it can happen that such a man might say to the headman that he would do best to veer off course a little while; and this is always heeded, for one realises then that he has seen *that* before the boat, which none of the others understand, but which can occasion misfortune — generally the draug in his half-boat, or a ghost.

One of Brogue Nils's many stories of that type had happened to an acquaintance of his, out on the winter fishings.

The weather had been thoroughly violent for a couple of days, but on the third day abated sufficiently that one of the boat crews that were staying in the fishermen's shed thought that it would surely be possible to take in their nets that day. The remainder were not prepared to try, however.

Now it is usual that the boat crews give each other a helping hand to push the boat out, and this was also to be the case now.

When they came down to the five-boarder, which had been drawn a good way inland, they found the oars and the thwarts turned backwards in the boat, and besides, despite all their united efforts it was impossible to move it from the spot. They tried once, twice, thrice without avail.

But then one of them, who was known to be a seer, said that from what he saw it would be best if they did not touch the boat again today; it was heavier than man's might.

With one of the boat crews that were staying in the fishermen's shed there was also a bright boy of fourteen, who used to amuse them all the time with all sorts of shenanigans and who was never still.

He took a huge stone and threw it with all his might into the stern of the boat.

Suddenly there then rushed out of it, visible to all, a draug in seaman's clothes, with a huge tangle of sea wrack instead of a head. He had turned everything backwards and weighed the boat down, and now rushed out into the sea so that the foam boiled around him.

After that had happened, the five-boarder slid smoothly into the water.

But the seer looked at the boy, and said that he should not have done that.

The boy, though, laughed as before and said that he did not believe in that sort of thing.

When they had come home then that evening, and the people were lying sleeping in the fishermen's shed, at about twelve o'clock at night they heard the boy shouting for help.

One of them also thought that by the gleam of the fading oil lamp he saw a huge hand reaching inwards from the door, up to the bunk where the boy lay.

The boy was already being dragged, screaming and resisting, across to the door, before the others came to their senses sufficiently to be able to take hold of him, to keep him from being dragged out.

But now a hard battle took place right in the doorway, as the draug pulled at his legs whilst the whole crew held onto his arms and body.

Thus, at the hour of midnight, moaning, he sawed to and fro in the half-open doorway, as now the people, now the draug had most of him.

All at once the draug let go, so that the whole crew fell inwards over each other onto the floor.

But the boy was dead then, and they realised that the draug had only then released him.

The following winter they heard a moaning at night, at twelve o'clock, down in the fishermen's shed. And there was only peace when it was moved over to another site.

— The same honour which the Østland farmer often places upon having the best trotting horse, the Nordlander places, probably equally heatedly, upon owning the boat which sails fastest.

A really exceptional boat is renowned there in the North in just as many villages as a really 'top' trotter in the South. Each is followed by its particular romanticism, which fills the villages with all kinds of legends about speed and wondrous races.

To build such a boat with the correct waterlines is a matter of genius, which cannot be imparted in theories; for it concerns a special sense for every individual boat on the part of the boat-builder. With simple copies it fares as elsewhere in life: they only ever sail moderately well. What it has cost the Nordlanders to eventually arrive at that shape of vessel which now enables them, in their small boats, nearly to fly before the wind from the enormous seas that foam behind them and which, if they reached the boat, would bury it under them — how many generations up there have suffered and struggled and thought about and corrected that design, under punishment of death for every mistake, in a manner of speaking — in short the history of the Nordland boat from the days of the generation that first took up the battle with the sea up there and until today — that is a forgotten Saga, full of the feats of the ordinary working man.

— One winter's evening in January, a little before the fishings began, I heard one of the people from the great boat crews that were overnighting with us then tell a tale. He had been started off by a couple of stories by Brogue Nils, and now he wanted to show us that even where he was from, namely down on Dønø in Helgeland, near Ranen, they had equally good kinds both of wondrous stories and of boats as we had up there.

The narrator was a little, glib fellow, who sat the whole time shifting and changing position on the bench whilst he narrated.

With his pointed nose and small, reddish, round eyes he resembled some uneasy sea bird on a skerry. Now and again he would interrupt himself by dipping into his lunch box, as if each time he drew out of it a new piece of the tale.

The story went thus:

On Kvalholm down in Helgeland there lived a poor fisherman, who was called Elias, with his wife Karen, who had earlier worked for the minister over at Alstadhaug.

They had raised a hut for themselves there, and now he went fishing off the Lofotens on 'daily rowings'.

Lonesome Kvalholm was not, though, free from being haunted. When the man was away his wife would hear all sorts of ghastly noises and screams, which could not come of anything good.

Every year saw another child, but they were both hard-working. When seven years had passed there were six children in the home; but that same autumn the man had also been able to scrape together enough that he thought he could now afford a six-oarer, and from now on go fishing in his own boat.

One day, as he was walking along with a fish-spear in his hand

and thinking this over, by a rocky outcrop down on the beach he chanced, unawares, on a monstrously big seal which was lying sunbathing right behind it, and which was probably just as surprised as was the man who was looking at it.

Elias was not slow, however; from the outcrop where he was standing he thrust the long, heavy fish-spear right down into its back, just beneath the neck.

But then there was a fuss! The seal at once rose onto its tail, right up in the air as high as a boat's mast, and looked at him with a pair of bloodied eyes so evilly and poisonously, simultaneously showing its teeth in a grin, that Elias nearly went out of his wits with fright. Then it suddenly swept into the sea so that its foaming collar lay filled with blood behind it.

Elias saw no more of it; but that same afternoon, into the landing place in Kvalvik where his house stood, floated the fish-spear with the iron spike broken off. Elias thought no more of this. That same autumn he bought his six-oarer, for which he had already put up a little boat-shed in the summer.

One night, as he lay and thought about his new six-oarer, it occurred to him that in order properly to look after his boat, maybe he ought to place another stay under each side to brace it.

He loved his boat so excessively that it was no trouble for him to get up with a lantern and go down to it.

As he now stood and illuminated it he suddenly glimpsed, dimly, in the corner across on a tangle of nets, a face which exactly resembled the seal's; for a while it grinned angrily at him and the light.

Its gape seemed to grow bigger and bigger, and then a large man rushed out through the boat-house door, but not too quickly, though, for Elias to glimpse by the gleam from the lamp that a long iron spike stuck from his back.

And now it was that he began to understand a thing or two.

But he was still more afraid for his boat than for his life.

The morning in January when he sailed out to fish, with two men in his boat besides himself, he heard in the dark a voice from a skerry just at the outlet of the cove. It laughed scornfully and said:

'When it's a five-boarder, then watch yourself, Elias!'

However, many years passed before it was to be a five-boarder for Elias, and his eldest son Bernt was then seventeen years old.

The autumn when this happened, Elias travelled with his whole family in his boat to Ranen, in order to trade in his six-oarer and thus with the balance to buy himself a five-boarder. At home was only a recently-confirmed Lappish girl, whom they had taken in several years before.

Now there was a boat, a little four-and-a-half compartment five-boarder, which he had in his sights then, and which the best boat-builder there had finished and tarred that autumn. He bought that against the six-oarer and a balance in money.

Elias intended now to sail home, but first stopped by at the trading post and supplied himself and his family with Christmas fare, and a little keg of brandy, besides.

Pleased as he was with his trade, he and his wife surely took a drop too many that day, and Bernt, their son, also got to taste a sip with them.

With that they now sailed the new boat homeward.

There was no other ballast in it besides himself, his wife and the children, as well as the Christmas fare.

His son Bernt sat at the prow, his wife, helped by the next-eldest son, held the halyard, and Elias himself sat at the helm, whilst the two youngest brothers, twelve and fourteen years old, were to take turns with the bailer.

They had fifty miles of seaway to sail, and when they left the fjord it became apparent that they would certainly come to test the boat the first time it was used. It gradually blew up to a storm, and combs of spray began to break in the heavy sea.

Now Elias really got to see what kind of boat he had: it coped like a sea bird amongst the waves, without so much as a splash in the boat, and from this he judged that he did not need to take in a whole reef, as any other, ordinary five-boarder would have to do in this weather.

Later in the day he saw, across on the sea not far away, another five-boarder with a full complement and four reefs in the sail, just as he had.

It set the same course, and he found it a little odd that he had not seen it before.

It appeared to want to race with him, and when Elias realised this he could not resist again putting out a reef.

Now they tore along like the arrow, past promontories, holms and skerries, so that Elias thought he had never been on such a proud voyage before, and now the boat also showed itself in its true colours, namely, that it was the best in Ranen.

The sea had become worse, meanwhile, and they had already shipped a couple of dangerous waves. They broke over the prow out front, where Bernt was sitting, and were sailed out again in the lee near the stern.

Since it had grown gloomier the other boat had kept quite close, and they were now so near to each other that they could have thrown a bailer over to one another.

Thus their paths continued abreast in steadily harder sea, out into the night.

The fourth reef ought really to have been taken in now, but Elias was reluctant to yield the sailing match and thought to bide as long as possible, until they reefed across in the other boat, where it must be required equally as much.

Now and again the brandy would still go round, for now there was both cold and damp to keep out. The phosphorescence, which was playing in the black waves by Elias's own boat, shone singularly strongly in the foam strip around the other, which seemed to be ploughing and upturning a drift of fire along its sides.

By the bright phosphor gleam he could even distinguish the rope ends across in it. He could also clearly see the people on board with their sou'westers on their heads; but since their weather side lay closest they all turned their backs, and were mostly shielded by the steeply-heeling side of the boat.

Suddenly a terrible breaker, whose white comb Elias had long glimpsed through the dark, broke over the prow, where Bernt was sitting. It was as if it stopped the whole boat for an instant, the boards quivered and shook under its pressure and then, when the boat — which for a moment lay heeled half-over — rose again and picked up speed, it streamed out over the leeward side aft.

Whilst this was happening he thought that there was a horrible screaming across in the other boat.

But when it was over, his wife, who was sitting by the halyard, said in a voice that cut him to his soul: 'Good God, Elias, that wave took Martha and Nils with it!'

They were their two youngest children, the first nine and the other seven years old, who had been sitting in the compartment near Bernt. To this Elias just answered: 'Don't let go of the halyard, Karen, or you'll lose more!'

Now the fourth reef had to be taken in, and when that was done, Elias found that he could well take in the fifth, too, for the weather was worsening; but if he were to sail the boat clear of the steadily heavier waves he did not dare, on the other hand, reduce his sail further than he really needed to.

However it turned out that the scrap of sail which they could set gradually became smaller and smaller. The sea smoked and drove in their faces, and eventually Bernt and the next-eldest brother, Anton, who until now had helped his mother over at the halyard, had to old on to the yard: an expedient which one resorts to when the boat cannot even cope with having the last reef set — here the fifth.

The companion boat, which had been away in the meantime, now suddenly reappeared at their side with exactly the same sails as Elias's boat. —

But now he was beginning not really to like the crew on board it.

The two who stood there and held the yard, and whose pale faces he glimpsed beneath their sou'westers, in the strange illumination of the breaking foam seemed to him more like dead men than people, and neither did they speak a word.

A little way to the windward side he again descried the high, white back of a new, towering wave which was coming through the dark, and he prepared himself in good time to meet it.

The boat was laid with its bow facing it obliquely and the sail was lowered as much as possible in order to get up enough speed to cleave and sail the wave out again.

The towering wave rushed in with a roar like a waterfall; again they lay for an instant heeled half-over; but when it was past, his wife no longer sat at the halyard, nor was Anton standing and holding onto the yard any longer — they had both gone overboard.

Also this time Elias thought that he heard that same horrible shout in the air; but in the middle of it he clearly heard his wife fearfully shouting his name.

When he grasped that she had been washed overboard he just said: 'In Jesus' name!' and then was silent.

He would most have liked to follow her, but also felt that it was now a matter of saving the rest of the load that he had on board, namely Bernt and the other two sons, the one twelve, the other fourteen years old, who for a while had been bailing, but who had since found space in the stern, behind him.

Bernt now had to manage the yard alone, so they both helped one another as much as possible.

Elias dared not let go of the tiller, and he held it fast with a hand of iron that had long been numb from exertion.

A while later the comrade boat again appeared; it had as before been away a while.

But now he also saw more of the huge man who sat aft in the same place as he. From out of his back beneath his sou'wester stuck, when he turned, rightly enough a six-inch-long iron spike, which Elias indeed thought he recognised.

But at this he now became quite clear of two things in his own mind; one was that it was none other than the draug himself who was steering his half-boat there right beside him and who had led him into damnation, and the other was that it was surely so ordained that he was sailing his last journey that night.

For he who sees the draug at sea is a doomed man.

He mentioned nothing to the others, so as not to sap their courage, but in silence committed his soul to the Lord.

During the past hours he had had to bear off course because of the storm. It began to snow thickly, too, and he knew that he would have to wait until dawn to sight land.

The journey meanwhile went as before.

Now and again the boys in the stern complained that they were freezing, but in the wet there was nothing to be done, and besides, Elias was thinking of quite different things.

He had acquired such a terrible desire to take vengeance, and what he would have done, had he not had his three remaining children's lives to defend, was with a sudden turn to have tried to ram and sink that damned boat, which still steadily kept at his side in scorn, and whose evil purpose he knew only too well.

If his fish-spear had been able to hit the draug before, so a knife or gaff surely must be able to now, and he felt that he would gladly give his life to strike a real blow against the draug, for he had so mercilessly taken from him those he held most dear in this world, and even wished to have more.

When it was three or four o'clock in the morning they again saw, sailing toward them through the dark, a foaming breaker of such a height that at first Elias thought that they must be close to land, in the vicinity of a surf.

But he felt clearly that across in the other boat someone laughed and said:

'Now your five-boarder will turn, Elias!'

The latter, who foresaw the mishap, now said aloud: 'In Jesus' name!' and then he bade his sons hold with all their might onto the withes by the rowlocks when the boat went under, and not let go until it was above the water again.

He let the elder go forward to Bernt; he himself held the younger close by his side, probably secretly stroked his cheek too, and ensured that he had a good hold.

The boat was literally buried under the drift of foam, and was gradually lifted up at the front, and then went under.

When it rose again from the water, with the keel in the air, Elias, Bernt and the twelve-year-old Martin lay holding onto the withes. The third of the brothers was gone, however.

Now they first of all had to slice through the shrouds on one side so that the mast could float up by the side, instead of violently disturbing the boat whilst underneath, and next they had to get up onto the uneasy hull and punch open the key hole in order to let out the air within, which was keeping the boat too high up in the water for it to be able to lie still.

After great exertion this was achieved, and Elias — who had climbed up onto the hull first — now also helped the other two up.

And there they sat that long, dark, winter's night, clinging convulsively with hands and knees to the hull, which was washed over by the waves time, time and again.

After the passage of but a couple of hours Martin, whom his father had supported the whole time as best he was able, died of exhaustion and slid down into the sea.

They had already tried many times to shout for help, but then gave it up since they realised that it was of no use.

Whilst the two were sitting there alone upon the hull, Elias said to Bernt that he saw no other outlook than that he himself would come to 'be with your mother', but that he had an enduring hope that Bernt would in any case still be saved, if he just held out now like a man.

Then he told him about the draug whom he had speared below the neck with his fish-spear, and how the draug had now avenged itself on him and would surely not give in 'until he was quits'.

It was nearing nine o'clock in the morning when the day began to dawn.

Then Elias handed Bernt, who was sitting at his side, his silver watch with its brass chain, which he had snapped in two to drag out from beneath his buttoned-up waistcoats.

He sat a while yet, but when it grew lighter Bernt saw that his father's face was deadly pale, his hair had parted in places, as usually happens before death, and the skin was chafed from his hands from holding onto the keel.

His son understood now that the end was nigh for his father, and wished, as much as the pitching would allow, to move across and support him, but when Elias noticed this he said:

'Just you hold on tight now, Bernt! In Jesus' name, I'm going to you mother,' and with this he threw himself backwards off the hull.

When the sea had got what it wanted, it became, as anyone who has sat upon a hull knows, calmer for a good while afterwards.

It grew easier for Bernt to hold on; and with the brightening day there came more hope, too.

The weather abated, and when it grew properly light he even thought he recognised where he was, and that it was just outside his own home, Kvalholm, that he was lying drifting.

Then he began to shout for help again, but hoped most for a current that he knew bore to land, at a place where a promontory on the island interrupted the incoming waves so that it was calm.

And he drifted closer and closer, and at last came so close to one skerry that the mast, which was floating at the side of the boat, stroked up and down the slanting rocks with the motion of the waves.

Stiff as his joints were from sitting and holding on tightly, he now managed with great exertion to climb up onto the skerry, where he was able to drag the mast up onto land and moor the five-boarder.

The Lappish girl, who was alone at home in the house, thought for a couple of hours that she could hear cries of distress, and when these continued she climbed up onto a rise to see what it could be.

Then she saw Bernt on the skerry and the upturned five-boarder scraping up and down against it. She ran down to the boat-shed straight away, pushed out the old four-oared boat and rowed it along the beach, around the island and out to him.

Bernt lay ill under her ministration the whole winter and did not go on the fishings that year.

It was thought, too, that after this he was a little strange in his ways now and again.

He never wished to go out to sea again, for he was sea-scared.

He married the Lappish girl and moved to Malangen, where he bought a piece of land to clear, and where he is now living and doing well.

Chapter 4
Among the Sprite Skerries

It was summer. Susanna and I were now in our seventeenth year, and it had been decided that we should be confirmed that autumn.

It was in that year that my father entangled himself in his unequal battle with the authorities, amongst them the bailiff and the minister, about whether our trading place should be a fixed port of call for the Nordland steamer.

For my father this was a matter of vital importance, and the discord about it, which after all concerned the whole district, was already growing quite bitter.

It was, too, not least in this connection that the bailiff had travelled that summer to visit the minister, who was a very influential man.

Outwardly, relations between my father and the minister were not quite broken yet, and it was indeed to exhibit this manifestly that my father even at that time was still invited over to the minister's a couple of times.

And the result of this was that my father and I were invited along one day on a sailing trip out to the Sprite Skerries, which lay ten miles away.

First there was to be fishing for a while, and then we were to dine on milk-rings at Gunnar's Place, a steading which was leased from the manse.

When the minister's white cabin boat with four men at the oars glided out of the bay it was always accompanied by a certain pomp, and there would usually be people standing on the shore then, watching. That day my father was also standing out on the step with his telescope. He had excused himself from going along in person, but on the other hand had tactfully let me go.

Inside the cabin at the rear, which was open because of the heat, sat the minister's wife and the bailiff's two ladies, and outwith it at each side sat the minister and the bailiff, smoking their silver-mounted meerschaums in cosy conversation — they had been friends since their days at university.

Susanna and I, together with the housemaid from Trondhjem, who was dressed up for the occasion, had places in the roomy bow.

The minister's wife insisted on keeping an eye on that part of her house that she had brought with her, an enormous food basket, a real portable pantry. The huge food basket and the thin minister's wife quite took up one of the benches, whilst the other two ladies in their starched attire completely filled up the rest of the cramped cabin.

Not a zephyr stirred, and a long, bright swell ran in the West Fjord. It lay immensely calm, sunbathing. The wonderfully clear air allowed the eye to see nearly into eternity across the mountain ranges, whilst a mirage — an upturned mountain with a house beneath it and a couple of blowing whales — performed adventures for us across the blue plain of the sea.

Now and again we met a sea bird swimming in the bright swell. In our wake an occasional porpoise would tumble.

A while before noon we sailed in among the Sprite Skerries and now set about fishing in calm waters; for it was decided that despite the food basket we should first earn our luncheon ourselves.

Outside the skerries the surf roared in the quiet day and shot out mighty, white rays with an undertow of many fathoms, as the sea drew its regular, deep breath.

Restless, Susanna leaned over the gunwale, so that the locks of her hair nearly dipped into her own picture in the water, in order to watch the fish in the transparent sea, gliding at fifteen to twenty fathoms' depth in and out of the seaweed across the green-white bottom and flocking around the lines with which the adults, with their double hooks, often hauled up two fish at a time.

She called me quite blind, in her enthusiasm, every time I could not see exactly the fish she meant. And indeed I was shortsighted, too, but Susanna's least movement interested me more than any fish at all.

The scenery was truly captivating. The white-painted cabin boat swayed above its picture as if it were hanging in the air.

Gunnar's Place was also dipped in the water, with its patch of field below and the birch hillside above and around it.

The air, which in the course of the day had become hazy from the heat, was filled with a leafy fragrance whose strength one only finds in the South after it has rained.

After the passage of barely an hour the pail was full of fish, so that we had a 'boiling', and now we put to land.

On the green just above the buildings the minister's wife had in the meantime had a table carried out, upon which, on the fine damask cloth, had been placed milk-rings. She had also cooked sour-cream porridge, and moreover, as far as there was place, loaded the table with dishes from the food basket.

But the wind and the stronger stuff probably made the bailiff's head a little fuzzy in the end. To the great horror of the minister's wife he told of how the minister, grizzled and strict as he sat there now, had in his youth been an extremely lively fellow, and that the two had played many a mad prank together.

When he grasped that he had made a *faux pax*, he made a serious toast in order to rectify matters, in which he hoped, for the sake of the district, that the minister would be sure to triumph over all the machinations of his scheming neighbour — here he was stopped in his speech by a meaningful look from the minister across to me, where I sat at the end of the table, — and then finished with some absent-minded words, which were supposed to round it all off.

I felt cold and clammy and was surely as pale as a corpse.

For my father's sake I thought I should keep up good appearances, but the food rose in my mouth so that I was incapable of downing another morsel.

I looked across to Susanna; she sat blushing red.

There was silence for a while, in which each surely sat and brooded in his thoughts over what had passed, until the drowsiness of the summer's day got the upper hand, and the minister and the bailiff, who were both wont to take an after-dinner nap, proposed that we should relax for an hour and each seek out a place in the shade.

After what had passed at table I felt altogether unhappily disposed. An opinion about my father had been allowed to be aired which was so outrageous that it was pure torture for me to remain in the company longer.

A little way beyond the house the hillside sloped inwards into a narrow valley with birches and willows on the ridges of both sides, and between them there ran over the flinty stones a mirror-clear, sparkling little burn where a trout or two smacked.

Whilst the others slept I walked up along this and lay down, to brood over my sorrow in solitude.

I do not know for how long I had lain thus; but when I looked up, Susanna sat there, deeply moved.

She thought that they had been horrible to me, she said, and then, as if she could not bear to see me distressed, she silently stroked my hair from my brow again and again.

There was a warmth in the little hand and an expression in her face, struggling with tears, that my temperament, so needful of love, could not resist.

I do not know how it happened, but just remember that I stood and pressed her vehemently up against me, with my cheek against hers, and bade her love me, just a little, and I would love her so endlessly for the rest of my life.

I recall, too, that she answered 'Yes', and that we were both crying at this.

A little later we stood hand in hand, smiling, and looked at each other.

There arose simultaneously a new thought in each of us: that, indeed, we were betrothed now.

Susanna was the first to voice this, and said, as she looked reassuringly at me with her faithful, deep, blue eyes, that from now on I must always remember that she loved me, though the others might be ever so horrible.

We heard them shout for us, and — something which before that day it would never have occurred to us to do — Susanna hurried ahead a little way alone, so that we returned to the company separately.

I already had the sun in my eyes late in the forenoon of the following day when Anna Kvæn, as had been her wont since I was a child, shook me awake, and told me that my father had left for Tromsø early that morning. He had been up in my chamber early, before he left, and when he came down again he had said of me that 'He was lying and smiling in his sleep and looked so happy, poor boy!'

It was sorely infrequently that a sympathetic word came from my father, and therefore these lodged in my memory.

My father was himself anything but happy at that time, though.

The aforementioned steamer controversy lay heavily on his heart, he wished now to try the last resort, namely to have the matter properly considered through the newspapers, and it was about this that he wished to address himself in person to an attorney in Tromsø.

These affairs of the house lay outwith my ken however.

Chapter 5
The Confirmation

That same autumn, during this state of affairs between our parents, Susanna's and my confirmation took place.

Since I was only enrolled late in the confirmation course it was arranged that, besides the meetings in the church every Monday, I should read alone with the minister on Fridays.

In his abrupt manner my father made a little private speech to me beforehand, in which he hoped that I would not put him to shame before the minister.

The readings up in the minister's study were a whole new spiritual development for me.

The great, grey-haired man, with that strong, broad face and those heavy silver spectacles, usually pushed up onto his brow above the heavy eyebrows, would sit on the sofa with his great meerschaum in his mouth and explain, whilst I, neatly dressed and attentive, would be seated in the chair on the opposite side of the table.

It became more and more clear to me that the minister must be an honest and veracious man, but in addition hard and strict; for he always spoke of our duties, and the fact that Grace could not be thought to be given to us that we might escape these.

Sometimes he would even get into the vein of making observations, hardly all of which were meant for me, however; they were usually all kinds of attempts to reason away the doubts which one might possibly have about the Articles of Faith, especially of the miracles — these he liked to explain in a natural way. In the course of this he could be extremely witty in his comparisons, and I used to believe then that, as in many traits in his strong-willed face when he was talking, I recognised Susanna's nature.

The small, pretty hands and fine, well-proportioned, if not especially tall figure she clearly had from her father too, and, besides, a certain toss of the head when what she said was to be more penetrating than usual.

But in addition Susanna had something warm and sudden, nearly volcanic, in her nature, which to me seemed to be unrelated to the expression that lay in the minister's cold, clear eyes of reason.

The minister praised me for thoughtfulness, but often repeated, to my great inner humiliation, that I had a way of lowering my eyes evasively, which I had to see to disinvest myself of.

The minister doubtlessly believed that I was exaggeratedly shy, perhaps too that I suffered from the knowledge of my father's relationship to him.

The thing was, however, that his keen ice-blue or grey eyes sometimes stared at me as if they were looking right through me and slicing me up like an orange, right through to my secret with Susanna.

I felt like a traitor, who was betraying his confidence, and I would depict to myself unpleasantly what he would think, once he knew all, of me, who whilst preparing for his own salvation had been able to sit so false and shameless before him.

Besides, during the reading of the catechism it became more

and more clear to me that my relationship to Susanna, as long as it was kept secret from her parents, was not right, and now with this palpable sin in my heart I was, moreover, cold-bloodedly and deliberately to go and kneel at God's table.

These scruples also haunted me at home, and in the end turned me into a true martyr. All sin, it said in the catechism, could be forgiven, except sin against the Holy Ghost.

The more deeply my imagination sank into pondering about this sort of mysterious crime against the Divine, which moreover stood outwith Grace and could not be forgiven, the higher within me rose the choking fear that the very sin which I was now consciously and with cold-blooded awareness in the process of committing might be of that kind.

My qualms especially concerned the sacraments of the altar, which I now shamelessly and quite purposefully intended to profane, thereby to hide the fact that I was deceiving the hand that offered me them.

In vain I sought to push these thoughts aside, or at least to defer thinking about them until the very last day before the confirmation.

My mind simply became more uneasy every day, and in my frightened imagination there loomed up things that no longer depended on my own will, but in which, horrified, I stood in the midst of all the possibilities and aspects of the fear of Hell.

I did not dare to calm myself by trying to engage Susanna in conversation about the matter; for as long as she did not know that what was now being carried out was sin, neither would she be at fault, and rather than plunge her into suchlike my lot was to stand alone with my burden.

To reveal all at the last moment to the strict minister would — notwithstanding that a child betrothal would lead, as I then thought, to an unbearable scandal for us both — only result in my losing Susanna; moreover I did not dare to do so without her consent. Everything was thus, to me, knotted together in a ring of impossibility, in which every way out was closed.

The last two Mondays that I stood in the church whilst the minister catechised us, I often looked sombrely across at Susanna. She stood there bonny, smiling and unaware; she suspected nothing, and indeed neither could she help.

During the days just before the confirmation my burden developed into a feverish condition, in which I was often hardly myself really, but felt awfully unhappy.

It seemed to me in the end that I was simply giving my salvation away for Susanna's sake. At night I would start, terrified, from dreams in which I saw myself kneeling at the altar with Susanna at my side — she looked so unsuspectingly, celestially delightful then — whilst the minister stood with a face of thunder, as if he sensed that a soul was now to be killed, and that in the Host, indeed, he was accomplishing the Lord's revenge.

Another night I awoke at a kind of scornful laughter under my bed, and with a vision-like conception that the Evil One lay curled up and menacing under it like a huge snake. I stayed under the quilt, with pounding heart, until early in the morning I heard people moving, down in the steading, and I risked fleeing from my bedroom. —

It was the day of the confirmation.

That morning, before it was time to go to church, I stood dressing myself in my new outfit in front of the mirror in the 'blue room', the room where my mother had been kept shut up for those many years she was ill.

I saw through the small-paned windows boat after boat, full of finely dressed confirmands, with their festively dressed parents, rowing in the clear autumn day in across the bay and landing, some at our jetty, some at the landing place by the manse.

This impression of solemnity suddenly filled me with despair. I thought of how all of them could enter the kingdom of God's salvation just as easily as they were now rowing into the sunny, clear bay on this calm Sunday morning, whilst I alone stood without hope of salvation.

It occurred to me all at once that in my sad, spiritually dark home I had essentially, since childhood, always had a deep feeling inside me that happiness and salvation were not meant for me, and that all of the real happiness and joy I had had up to now had actually just been borrowed sunshine from the manse.

With the sin that I bore, even Susanna I could only have on loan until I died, when we would after all have to separate, and I return to the evil powers of misfortune that from my earliest moments here in my home had seemed to take me into their possession.

I turned to the wall and wept.

When I was to continue dressing again, and cast a glance at the mirror, it was without fright, indeed with a certain calm, that my gaze fixed on that old vision from my childhood: the lady with the rose, whom I saw standing behind me in the open door to my chamber, pale, and sorrowfully looking at me, until all at once she was gone.

The church bells were ringing, and the people streaming towards the church. That day Anna Kvæn and all the inmates of our house also went to church. Father accompanied me, and in passing obligingly greeted the minister when they met at the entrance.

The order in which we confirmands were to stand in church had been decided last Monday. I was to stand at the top on the boys' side, just as Susanna on the girls' side.

A hymn had already been sung before Susanna came, accompanied by her mother and dressed like an adult in a black silk dress with gauze about her throat and arms and a locket on her breast. She remained sitting in the manse pew with her mother until the gripping sermon was over.

I must surely have looked very ill and worn out, for when the minister began the catechisation with me he paused in the middle of the question, with an expression as if he wanted to ask what was wrong with me.

I answered correctly, and with a nod he then went across to Susanna, who was standing there with hands folded and looking down, with tear-stained cheeks and rather pale with excitement, before the question came.

Whilst her father was catechising her she looked up at him with those blessed blue eyes, so innocent and full of confidence that it was more than clear that at that moment there was in her not a trace of bad conscience.

When it was undergone, and her father went further down the floor, she smiled, relieved yet seriously, across at me, as if I were the other proper person whom she had at that moment to turn to.

Insofar as I could I looked unnoticed across at her as she stood there erect and delightful, with her rich hair put up in adult style.

Now and again she looked across at me, too, but then I avoided her.

For me her gaze was now just one more sin, just as every holy word I heard was but an addition to my burden of sin — effecting the opposite of blessing.

The service lasted a long time, and the nervous over-exertion had the effect, as it later so often has had with me, of making my head swim and all before my eyes grow black with dark points. There appeared, to my horror, a dark spot everywhere that I cast my eye, and I thought in distress that this must already be the beginning of damnation.

I dared not look across at Susanna now, lest I put the mark on her, and in the end I could not resist inspecting the floor where I stood, for possible burnt marks under my feet.

I thought of the Sea-Man, who in the church in Vaagen had enticed the minister's daughter with him, and whose instinct had driven him out of church during the Blessing, whilst I was doomed to remain.

After the Vow was finished I remember dimly that there was another talk and hymns were sung.

When I later found myself walking along the way home with my father, who was supporting me, wearing a worried expression, my last memory of it all was that Susanna, who had presumably realised that I was ill, towards the end of the church service had looked at me with exactly the expression that the lady with the rose had that same morning — still, pale, melancholy, like someone who so much wishes to help, but cannot.

I believe that what my father had said to me about not letting him down in front of the minister contributed no little to my holding myself upright to the last, for I fainted no sooner than we had entered the living-room at home, and was taken to bed whilst my father, who had become seriously frightened, immediately sent an express messenger for the doctor.

When the physician came the next day he found me in a violent delirium.

My imagination flowed like an undammed river, with a stream of the most confused ideas.

It seemed to me that figures from Hell were dancing and nodding around my bed, amongst whom one with a long letter of condemnation with a seal under it, and that Anna Kvæn was rolling her glowing eyes, whilst Susanna would look at me now and again with an agonised expression, as if it were not in her might to prevent my loss.

From what I later learnt the physician to begin with thought that it was a nervous fever, but from certain symptoms and the contents of my imaginings, about which Anna Kvæn, who probably had her own thoughts on the matter, felt it essential to inform him, he changed his opinion entirely.

He had treated my poor mother during her mental illness and now rediscovered precisely the same conception of the lady with the rose, and fear of evil powers, in me, her son.

Three weeks after this I was, although pale and worn out by the lengthy nervous paroxysms, completely fit again.

The whole millstone of the burden of sin was as though lifted from my breast, and I received Communion without a trace of scruples.

I also felt like a completely worthy person when, the following Sunday, in my black dress coat I went on a confirmand's visit to the manse.

On this occasion Susanna — I think a mite on parade for me — was sitting like an adult at her own sewing table on the elevation by the window. But when her mother went out for currant wine and cake, at her beckoning I had hastily to review her costly sewing table with all its drawers, both those above and those which appeared beneath when she pushed the upper drawers aside.

In one of these latter, which she opened with a rather mischievous look but shut lightning-fast again as soon as her mother came in, there lay the brass ring with the glass stone in it which she had once been given by me, and at its side a couple of old notes from our childhood years, which I recognised.

When I left, my heart leapt inside me; for I had unexpectedly had a tryst in which the faithful conviction of Susanna's heart had shown itself to me more strongly than any verbal assurance.

It occurred to me that something must have happened at home of late, for my father's terse, cold way of treating me had markedly changed. In this connection he had made me a present of a double-barrelled gun in a seal-skin holster, and a watch, and himself had suggested that for the days until I left, Jens Prentice and the four-oared boat should be at my disposal as often as I wished to go out and shoot or fish.

What had happened became clear to me when the doctor turned up one day and asked if he could accompany me up to my room.

The bald, stocky little doctor, with his homespun jacket and steel-framed spectacles on his stubby nose, was one of those hardly physicians of our fjord districts who laid great store by travelling in all sorts of weather. One always saw him in the best of moods when he had just come in from a storm.

He was a decisive and straightforward man whose word instinctively inspired confidence, and he had in addition something warm and ingenuous in his manner which enabled him, when he so wished, to be sorely winning.

He was the house physician both for us and the minister, and an intimate friend of both families.

When we came up to my room he bade me sit and listen to him, whilst, as was his wont, he determined a route for himself on the floor, where he could walk to and fro with his hands behind his back whilst he was talking.

He had, he said, carefully weighed up whether he should remain silent about what he had on his heart, or talk to me, just as he was doing now, but he had resolved to do the latter, since my recovery depended upon my being absolutely clear about what it was I was suffering from.

My recent illness had, at least in part, been an outbreak of a disposition to mental illness which he knew was inherited in our family, on my mother's side, yet further stages back. That this outbreak had now materialised in me had surely only been because I had all too strongly given myself up to all kinds of influences upon my imagination, linked to the life of idleness he knew I always led at home.

The only means to halt the development of this disposition was to work, with a fixed, determined goal ahead of me — for example to study, which he believed was in my nature — and in addition a healthy lifestyle too: long walks, hunting, fishing, friends and interests; but no more idleness, no more exacting novels, no more unhealthy dreams. He had spoken to my father about this and recommended my travelling to the seminary at Trondenæs as a suitable preparation for study, which would moreover effect the necessary interruption of my present life.

When the doctor left me a while later I remained sitting in my room, with a serious, moved heart.

To have thus become transparent to myself and to have my mystery solved was an extraordinary relief to me, indeed I can say that it was a turning-point in my life.

The feeling of being spiritually unwell, which, like a quiet

impression on my mind, a sense of unhappiness always, for as long
as I could remember had lain in the background of my soul —
even if suppressed in the brighter summertime of my relations
with Susanna — was thus not sin, not the weight of crime, not a
mysterious, dark exception in me from all the rest of nature's
order, but just an illness, purely and simply an illness, which was
to be treated with an equally natural cure!

I would not have believed that anyone could sit as happy as if he
had received good tidings while hearing that he was mad, or at
least in danger of becoming that; but now I know that even that
can happen in this world.

I prayed now, so it seemed to me, for the first time in my life
easily and confidently to my God, to whom I did after all stand in
the same relationship as all others, and if there were any difference
then only so much the closer, for I was a poor, sick person.

I felt as if God's sunshine, after a long, heavy day of rain had
again broken forth over me. I prayed for myself, for Susanna, for
my father, and in the enjoyment of this new, sure relationship I
continued to pray first for everyone at home, then for those in the
manse, then for the sacristan and finally, for want of others, just as
in church for 'All who are ill or sorrowful', amongst whom, glad at
heart, I now counted myself.

Chapter 6
At the Sacristan's

It was just two days before I was to travel to Trondenæs with a
sloop, which lay ready to go north.

Whilst, at a loss, I weighed up all kinds of possibilities of being
able to talk to Susanna yet one more time before I was to leave, a
message came to me from the sacristan that I definitely had to

come and see him the next day, at eleven o'clock sharp; he would not be home later.

The same forenoon that the message came, Susanna had been at the sacristan's. She had, without saying a word, sat down by the table with her face buried in her arms.

When the rather taken aback sacristan entreated his 'poppet', as he called her in his anxiety, she had eventually looked up at him with a face wet from tears and said that she was weeping because she was so totally, totally unhappy.

'But *why*, dear Susanna?'

'Because' — suddenly exploded about his ears — 'I love David and he loves me, and we're betrothed, but no-one may know of it except you, sacristan! — and you wouldn't betray us?'

With this last question she threw herself, weeping, around the neck of the sacristan, who, dazed and bewildered by this news, in his heart already felt won over long before he even had any idea of what he was agreeing to.

He sat Susanna down in a chair, talked to her and comforted her for a while, until he had managed to arrive, in his own mind, at the reasonable answer that we ought to use the coming two years of separation as trial years, and therefore in that time not even write to one another.

But the sacristan then had to promise in return that we should be allowed to meet the following forenoon for a moment at his house, for a final meeting and farewell, and also that during the time I was away the sacristan was to to tell her everything that he learnt about me.

When I came to the sacristan's the next day I found him sitting in his chair, sorely sombre and concerned, leaning forward with his arms on his knees and staring down at the sand floor, which was strewn with sprigs of spruce as though for a festival.

My arrival did not seem to disturb him in his observations, although a little nod at my entrance had shown me that I had at least been noticed.

He slowly sung his violin to and fro in front of his knees, with a soft pinch of the strings at each pass, so that it reminded one of a muffled church bell. His mild, grey eyes glided across to me with a meditative, scrutinising gaze, as if he were actually seeing me now for the first time, and a faint smile showed that the inspection had not turned out quite so badly, either.

A little later the door was shadowed, and to my surprise in stepped Susanna.

She walked hastily and blushing right up to me and took my hands with the words:

'Dear David, the sacristan knows all; he has allowed us to say farewell here.'

'Yes, I have indeed, children!' said the sacristan, 'but only for a moment, because Susanna pleaded so much for it, and in order that you both could hear what I think about it all, after weighing it up.'

He now gave a little talk, in which he said that he did not see anything wrong in our loving one another, although we were, to be sure, absurdly young.

That we had not disclosed our relationship to our parents, he hoped — and he had thought long over this — was also excusable, since they would hardly even give the matter at all its proper seriousness, and we might thus just have our feelings hurt.

He did not intend to be an intermediary for secret love letters, as Susanna had asked him to be, and this was both for his own sake and for ours, as we ought to use the coming two trial years to see if there really were truth in our love, or if it were just childish fancy of the kind that would later evaporate from our minds again.

With that pronouncement the old sacristan good-naturedly left the room.

When we were alone, Susanna told me, whispering, why she had risked confiding in the sacristan.

For she had heard at home that he had at some time in his youth had an unhappy love, and that this was the reason why he had never wished to marry later, and had become so strange.

Next, in eager haste she drew from her pocket — she was still wearing her old blue-checkered, short, everyday dress, which was to be worn out, but with an 'adult' hairstyle — a cross made of small blue glass beads, which I was to wear around my neck closest to my breast on a silken thread, which she also drew from her pocket.

From her pocket, that held so much, she then with some difficulty drew a small pair of scissors.

Now it was a matter of a lock of my hair, precisely that black one at my temple, which she had long had an eye on, she said, and which she intended to keep in the space inside her confirmation locket.

When I then in return asked for a lock of hers, which I too had 'long had an eye on', she said this was not necessary, since the cross of pearls I had been given was threaded on her own hair.

Then there was something I had to promise her, and which she had thought through whilst sitting at home and sewing, for she would think of so much then.

It was that when I became a student I should present her with a betrothal ring of gold, with the inscription:

David and Susanna

on one half of the inside, and on the other side there should be written:

Like David and Jonathan.

It was our parents' disagreement that had brought her to this idea.

'But,' she broke off, 'you're not even listening to me, are you, David?'

Indeed, I was really standing thinking of something else; it was whether I might dare kiss her as a farewell; I remembered that summer, out among the Sprite Skerries.

Just then there was a scrape out in the stone hall in front of the door, which meant that the sacristan thought it would be soon enough now, and Susanna immediately made haste, to my disappointment, to ensure that the presents, which I still stood holding in my hand, were hidden down in my breast pocket.

She had just finished this when the sacristan stepped in and said that we must now say farewell to each other.

Susanna looked at the sacristan for a moment and thence, pale and with eyes filling with tears, over to me, as if the thought that we were to part had only now really occurred to her.

She made an impetuous movement — she obviously wanted to embrace me, but then reined herself in as the sacristan was present.

Now she just took my hand, raised it to her eyes without saying a word, and hurried away.

It was more than I could endure, and I believe it was too much for the old sacristan as well. He walked back and forth and quietly pinched the strings, whilst across at the table I let my tears run freely.

Before I left he played a delightful little 'air', which he had composed when he was twenty.

It touched me deeply, for I thought it seemed to be about me and Susanna; it sang within me for long afterwards, so that I learnt it by heart.

'There is another part, too,' he said when he had finished, and then — after a little pause as if in a burdensome reminiscence — 'but it's not very merry, and does not suit you!'

When the sloop left, early the following morning, a kerchief waved from the hall window of the manse, and in reply a shining hat on deck.

Chapter 7
Trondenæs

On a promontory on the northern side of Hindø in Senja lies Trondenæs church and manse.

This church was once Christianity's northernmost frontier fortress, and has stood there, mighty, with its white towers, the far-reaching peal of its bells and its holy song, like an immense bishop in a white surplice, bearing St Olaf's Christian consecration and altar candles into the darkness amongst the Finmark trolls.

I dwell on the recollection of this church and its surroundings because I was, in the two years I spent at Trondenæs, so strongly influenced by the mighty impression on the imagination that the place has. The hollow ground with its reputed underground vaults was like a concealed abyss to me, filled with secrets, and in the church, whose silence I often sought, the daylight sometimes cast shadows in the passages and recesses as if beings from another time were on the move.

I read Latin and Greek with great progress with the amiable, erudite minister in whose house I was living, and the other school subjects with one of the seminary's teachers. But in my free moments I would seek out those places that to such a high degree occupied my imagination, and Trondenæs was thus anywhere but the right place for my sickly mind.

My overwrought nervous state has, as I have later noticed, a connection with the phases of the moon. At such times those places would exert an almost irresistible, compelling influence on me; I would steal unnoticed into their loneliness and might sit there for hours, plunged into the many things that were vaguely created by my power of fancy, amongst them Susanna's delicate shape, which I sometimes thought seemed to float towards me, without my ever really being able to see her face, though.

It was late in the spring of the second year I was there that, in the middle of the day, under the influence of a sickly, moody, period like that, I was sitting inside the church on an elevation near the main altar deep in thought, with Susanna's blue cross in my hand.

My eye fell on a large dark picture on the wall at the side of the altar, which I had often seen without its having left any further impression. It represents, in life size, a martyr flung into a thorn bush whose pointed thorns, long as daggers, pierce his body at various places, and who, besides, dares not complain since a huge, painful thorn goes in under his throat and out of his open mouth.

This expression on his face suddenly became quite awful to me.

It was looking at me with an expression of quiet understanding, as if I were his comrade in suffering, who was to lie there when, at some time, his struggle eventually came to an end. It was impossible to take my eyes from it; it seemed to come alive, now moved quite close, now far away, into a murkiness created by my own dizzy mind.

It was as if in that picture the curtain were drawn aside from a piece of my own soul's secret history, and it was only with an effort of will, called forth by the fear of being sucked too far into my own imagination, that I managed to tear myself loose from it.

When I turned, in the light falling from the window near the topmost pew stood the lady with the rose.

She was wearing an expression of endless melancholy, as if she well knew the link between me and that picture, and as if the thorn twig in her hand were just a miniature of that same thorn bush in which the martyr lay yonder.

In the lonesome silence of the church an unutterable terror of invisible powers suddenly overcame me, a panic dread, in which I hastily fled out.

When I came out, I discovered that I had lost Susanna's blue cross. It could only be lying in the church, by the elevation where I had been sitting.

At that moment, whilst the terror was still seething in my blood, I would not have gone back in the church for any price in the world — except for Susanna's blue cross.

I found it, as I looked in complete calm on the floor where I had been sitting.

The other time in those years that my nervous system revealed its sickliness was in the back end of that year, a few months before I was to travel home.

Whilst he was inside with the minister, a farmer had tied a horse that was glass-eyed to the churchyard wall. I stood a while and looked at it; but afterwards its dead, expressionless gaze pursued me all day in my memory. It seemed to me that its eyes saw, instead of outwards, inwards into that world invisible to us, and as if it might naturally occur to it, when one forgot to watch the reins, to veer from the usual country road and onto the road to the other world, where the dead ply.

As I sat with this in my thoughts that afternoon at the minister's, where all sorts of things would be discussed, there suddenly stood before me a face from home, pale and strained, and little by little it became clear to me that the man to whom it belonged was fighting desperately to clamber out of the rough surf and up onto a rock.

It was none other than our lad Anders.

He fixed his half glass-, half horn-like gaze on me whilst he lay there, seemingly prevented from escaping by something down at his feet, which I did not see. He was wearing an expression as if he wanted to say something to me.

The vision only lasted an instant; but a painful, almost unendurable feeling that at that moment an accident had happened at home drove me out of my room and to roaming about uneasily in the fields for the rest of the day.

When I returned they asked me what had troubled me, since I had suddenly rushed out of the room, chalk-white.

A fortnight later came a sad letter from home. My father's sloop *Hope*, which, as was normal in those days, was uninsured, and was largely loaded with fish that my father had bought on his own account, had gone under on a trip to Bergen, in a storm in the Statt Sea.

The vessel had sprung a leak, and late in the afternoon had had to be landed. The crew had escaped with their lives, but our lad Anders had had both of his legs crushed.

This shipwreck was the first considerable loss to my father's fortunes. The second would come in the following year with the loss too of the other sloop, *Unity*, and a third blow, which was to be decisive for the future, struck when it was eventually decided by the Government that our trading place would not be a port of call for the steamer.

Chapter 8
At Home

In the month of December I was home again, where I found everything outwardly as of old, only, if possible, because of what had passed even quieter and sadder.

My father was restlessly active, but hardly communicative. Nor did he presumably look upon me as suitable to partake in his worries.

Susanna, who now like myself was more than nineteen years old, was on a visit at a family a number of miles away, and would only return home at Christmas.

My longing for her was indescribable.

It was in the last, dark, storm-filled week before Christmas that the Spanish brig *Sancta Maria*, forced in by a storm, lay to in the vicinity of our house in a fairly damaged condition, which meant that it had to lie for nearly six weeks being repaired, with our poor facilities.

The captain, who owned both the ship and its cargo, was a tall, yellow, finely-dressed Spaniard with somewhat grey-flecked hair, black eyes and heavy features. With him was his son, Antonio Martinez, a handsome young man with an olive-brown face and fiery eyes like his father.

My father had performed considerable services for señor Martinez during the salvage, and now with Nordland hospitality bade him give us the pleasure of his company.

Although communication between us could not be particularly lively, since the foreigners only understood a few words of Norwegian and otherwise had to make use of an interpreter, it did soon become evident that they were two very good-natured people. Their main occupation consisted of rolling and smoking cigarettes all day and overseeing the work on the brig.

The dark time has a depressing effect on the moods of many people there in the North, especially on those days when one is less busy.

Thus over Christmas, and especially on Christmas Eve itself, my father was always wont to be extremely sad. Whilst there was merrymaking in the whole house and the servants, dressed for the festival, were celebrating at the kitchen table, which was decorated with three-branch tallow lights, he would as a rule sit deep in thought in his office and not wish to be disturbed by anyone.

This Christmas Eve, however, for the sake of señor Martinez he was in the room for a while, but remained silent and dejected the whole time, as if he were simply longing for his lonesome office, to which he indeed withdrew right after supper.

Chapter 9
The Christmas Visit

That winter around Christmas there was a great number of foreigners around our way, mostly ships' captains who, because of the unsettled weather or sea damage, were staying at various places on land.

Besides, dignitaries had come from the South on public business.

A consequence of this was also a number of social gatherings, in which the hosts sought to outdo one another in their generous hospitality.

We had thus been invited to a Dinner and Ball on the third day of the New Year by the wealthy sheriff Røst, with whom the gentlemen from the South were staying for a while.

It was just ten miles for us to travel, but many others had as many as thirty or fifty miles to go, of which a considerable distance was seaway.

Røst's spacious property could house a whole crowd of guests, but this time, in order to provide overnight lodgings for the many visitors, he had in addition commandeered the neighbouring steading.

As I proceed to recount that visit, which was to be so filled with events and mental turmoil for me, I have promised myself to be brief, and I shall thus skip over many a feature and many a sketch which belong to a more complete picture of life up there.

According to the invitation we were to eat at three o'clock, but most of the boats arrived two or three hours in advance. Whilst the ladies were changing upstairs, the gentlemen gathered below in a deliberately dimly-lit room, where there was a 'bite to eat' and a schnaps, which might well be required after the journey.

There, in addition, they were made known to one another by the considerate host.

There was a long and fruitless wait for the minister and his ladies, and in the end it had to be decided to go to the dinner table without them.

The doors were now thrown open to the great, festively-lit dining-hall above, the guests streamed up the stair and, after much pausing at the doors and long, polite disputations about the order of rank, took their places around the great, heavily-laden, horseshoe table, which was resplendent with an unbroken row of wine bottles, three-armed candlesticks, tall centre-piece cakes and, especially right up at the place of honour, with a real pile of heavy silverware.

For the minister and his family three places were reserved among the dignitaries.

My father sat at señor Martinez' side up at the top table, and I in my modesty sat further down at one of the side tables.

The dinner party was of the good old congenial sort, which is now going more and more out of fashion everywhere. Certainly, one ate with a knife and had no silver forks; but on the other hand there was true merriment in the company, and for a long time afterwards one would have food for many a humourous conversation.

In the beginning, whilst one still sat with that freezing feeling of the white cloth, and overwhelmed by the impression of festivity, all was indeed very constrained.

Neighbours hardly even risked whisper to one another, and the begowned young ladies, who as if by some magnetic attraction had all ended up beside one another, sat for a long time in deeply discomfited silence all in one row, like a blue, red and white flowering hedge in which no bird dared sing.

The dinner was begun by the host bidding the guests welcome.

Next, in a couple of longer, considered speeches he proposed toasts to the dignitaries present, who in turn replied.

With this everyone felt that the proper, official threshold to enjoyment had now been crossed.

The host now, with lightened breast, entered into the much shorter and sweeter toasts to those absent — amongst whom were first and foremost the 'amiable minister and his family'.

At this toast it was not just I who noticed that my father left his glass untouched.

Meanwhile the dishes went round, and as the level of the wine of the bottles sank, the merriment rose.

Many a quick and bright head emerged now, having found its true field of battle, and the cross-fire, saturated with wit, mirthful sallies and amusing speeches — these latter most often in the form of stories with a sometimes perhaps rather drastic point — gave a vivid impression of that peculiarly Nordland humour.

The fact that when one was supposed to leave the table there were several who could not get up from their seats, and others who were later missing as a result of the battle, was simply what normally happened in get-togethers then.

Amongst the latter, unfortunately I was to be counted too.

The impression of the moment has always had a great power over me, and unused as I was both to this sort of merriment and to strong drink, I had inadvertently given myself up to the happy mood that flowed all around me.

I believe that I had never laughed as much in my whole life together as I had at that single dinner.

Diagonally opposite me sat the red-haired trader Wadel with his long, deadpan face, firing off one witty grenade after the other, and at my side whispered the hunchbacked clerk Gram, who was widely renowned for his good head and feared for his biting tongue. His piquant characterisations of the various people who were sitting at the table rose in malice the more he drank, and, had his words been heard, many a beaming face at the table would surely have changed its expression.

I also believe that besides this, he amused himself on the sly too by getting me inebriated; at least, he was always untiring in filling my glass, especially when the dessert wine was served.

His swift, shrewd, viper's eyes and some whispered words focussed my now otherwise thoroughly befogged attention on many a comic scene.

It seemed to me in the end that the room and table rose and fell, as if we were sitting in a sea swell in a great cabin.

Unclearly I can still see how later on, in the sailing hall, everyone squeezed past one another in two contrary streams around the table, between the wall and the chairs, to thank the host.

After all this I remember nothing until I awoke in pitch darkness, as if from a heavy, confused dream, and felt that I was lying in a soft eiderdown bed. Little by little, what had passed dawned in my memory, and I realised that I had been put to bed in one of the

72

guest rooms in the neighbouring steading. Whilst I lay pondering over this and feeling enormously unhappy, the elder señor Martinez came in to see me, with a light in his hand, to see how I was.

It then turned out to be past two o'clock in the morning, and to the fact that I had therefore slept for six or seven hours at one stretch I attributed, reasonably, my no longer feeling physically ill any more; all the more did I suffer morally, from a feeling of shame.

As far as I could make out, whilst I dressed, the neighbouring steading had indeed become a proper field hospital for the same sort of the victims of the dinner as was I, and amongst them I noticed, with a certain vengeful joy, the clerk Gram, my hunchbacked, malicious neighbour.

Señor Martinez demonstrated to me with all kinds of elated gesticulations that everyone was now enjoying the dance, and that I should be there too.

The thought that by now Susanna must have come a long time since and must have been waiting in vain, all at once shot through my mind like a lightning bolt.

How I could have forgotten her, even if only for an instant, was a mystery to me; but that I *had* done it lay heavily upon me.

The dining-hall had now been transformed into a ballroom, and the dancing had already been going on merrily for several hours to the full accompaniment of violin, clarinet and violincello.

At an opportune moment, in the middle of a dance, I stole in unnoticed.

As I stood there in my tight white gloves, pale and embarrassed, down by the open door through which the heat was streaming out into the cold passage like a fog, I suffered strongly to begin with from the feeling that everyone was about to look at me and think of my less-than-appropriate behaviour.

However the couples were swinging past one after the other, so close that the ladies' dresses touched me, and I began, insofar as my shortsightedness allowed, gradually to orientate myself in the hall.

The minister's wife sat on the sofa at the top, amongst several elderly ladies, in animated conversation with the bald-headed little doctor.

The minister was probably playing cards downstairs — but of

73

Susanna I saw nothing.

Up in the hall just then the young Martinez, with a beaming smile, was swinging a strikingly pretty lady, dressed in white with a blue, fluttering sash around her waist, in the polka.

She had heavy, delightful hair, which fell in gold, with a large silver pin like a spear through the nape, and a delicate garland on top.

She was looking down at the floor whilst she danced.

The lady was taller and fuller than Susanna, but had a distinctive charm to her figure that reminded me of her.

The light, almost nobly exquisite manner in which she directed her little feet in the dance — it was as if she were floating — was also like her, and therefore I followed the couple with an unconscious interest.

My shortsightedness prevented me from discerning clearly, and when they came past me the lady's bowed head was moreover shielded by her own arm, which trustingly leant up to the shoulder of the obviously happy Martinez.

What I saw was just a broad, pure, blessed brow, of which there could only be one in the world, and that a lock of her hair had fallen down and was playing about those white, round shoulders.

I felt myself shaking at the knees. This tall, fine, noble, lady could surely not possibly be Susanna!

With a feeling of jealousy, I fixedly watched them dancing until they came past the next time.

Just opposite me her eyes opened wide in laughter; her gaze fell right on me, and a powerful blush suddenly flooded over her face and shoulders right down to the lace edge of her dress.

It was Susanna!

In the little over two years we had been apart her beauty had unfolded in a wondrously rich manner. From the fine, seventeen-year-old bud had sprung forth in that short time a glorious, fully-grown woman.

The couple took their places at the top of the hall, near the row of elderly ladies.

I realised now that the two were about to dance the last long dance of the ball, the cotillion, which as a rule one tends to alternate with an eternity of circuits, and the thought raced through my mind that the young Martinez had probably been a success with Susanna the whole evening, since he was to be her partner in precisely this dance.

I became aware that the minister's wife visibly favoured him, and it occurred bitterly to me that he was, indeed, both a rich man and moreover, although shorter in stature than I, looked much more adult and manly.

To me it was like a knife in the heart. I had, then, lain drunk like a beast and let a stranger take Susanna from me.

With wild jealousy I noticed how the handsome, silent Martinez, talking with his black, fiery eyes, laughing and with all kinds of vivid nods and gestures sought to illustrate to her a new dance, which was to begin now; how he would sometimes bow over her, seeming to whisper confidingly, and how she would in turn look up from her place to him and laugh merrily, as only Susanna could laugh.

He took her by the hand and persuaded her to make an essay on the floor in front of their places, and this appeared to be even more amusing.

The young Martinez was obviously occupying her, and our old relationship was thus only childish play, which the grown-up lady now rather wished forgotten.

After our agreement to the two trial years, everything between us in that respect was after all quite clear, so that like adults, for that matter, we could now at the occasion converse easily and laughing about the whole thing.

My blood rushed to my head, and I felt that I had to avenge myself.

Before I had properly considered how, on a sudden impulse I began to converse animatedly, in such a way that it would appear that I was paying court to trader R.'s pretty daughter, who had just come to stand right beside me.

When Susanna, later in the new circuit, danced past us, she looked at me enquiringly and rather surprised.

The next time she came back, she inadvertently dropped her pocket handkerchief just where I was standing.

I picked it up, stiffly walked across and delivered it to the minister's wife, who, though — whether it was on account of my behaviour at the dinner table or of something else — received me strikingly shortly and coldly. I bowed to her just as coldly and then turned back to my old place, where I resumed my interrupted, laughing conversation with Miss R.

A while later Susanna swung past again, and she looked at me then with a serious yet uncertain expression, as if she were not really quite sure in her own mind what she should think; after that, she deliberately cast her eyes down every time.

I discovered to my satisfaction that Martinez actually danced clumsily. Whilst I laughed and conversed with my beautiful partner with forced exuberance, I was secretly tempted to place my foot in all inconspicuousness a mite maliciously forward, so that he might stumble over it.

And I do not quite know how it came about, but when Martinez danced past the next time he fell his length along the floor, and landed hard, too. He had been chivalrous enough in falling, though, not to use the support he could have had of his lady, so that Susanna was only half pulled down.

He rose and looked furiously across at me, the innocent cause of the mishap, who was standing apparently much too absorbed in my partner even to have noticed what had happened at all.

But the look which was sent from him for the one he gave me probably revealed, involuntarily, the whole truth to him; for he was about to rush straight up to me when he was unexpectedly stopped by Susanna, who, admittedly a little pale, stepped into his path, and with the bearing of a lady of the world calmly proffered her arm, that he might lead her further.

As Susanna was walking up arm in arm with the limping Martinez she suddenly turned her face to me with an expression so beaming with joy that I was suddenly carried, from my profound doubt, into the happiest, most jubilant certainty.

She had clearly understood that Martinez' accident was vengeance from my side for her sake, and had thereby had the doubt that my conduct during the past hour must have given her lifted from her breast; for she had soon perceived that I was not inebriated, and coquetry was all too distant from her own candid, veracious nature for her to be able to understand such in me. In all truth, she really was just a refined, feminine edition of her father's strong nature.

I went and made the most persevering apologies to the young Martinez for my clumsiness, whilst Susanna was sitting at his side and listening, until he, good-natured as he basically was, eventually let himself be mollified.

He grew rather long in the face, though, when Susanna immediately afterwards suggested that I should dance the coming circuit with her, in order that he could rest his bruised leg for the following one.

Yes, I danced with her, that pretty, full-grown woman in the white ballgown, whom I had not recognised a while earlier because her own wonderfully developed beauty had concealed her.

We had taught one another to dance, and I believe we both danced unusually well. That delicate garland with small, white flowers between green leaves accentuated her rich hair; I had my arm around her waist and felt her lithely leaning up against me, whilst she swayed with me in the dance, happy and secure as a child.

Her brow was near my lips, and our gazes, which sought one another's during the dance, spoke again and again of how delightful it was to meet, when we had been yearning dearly for one another for two long years.

When I led her back to her place I received a handshake and a look which entirely indemnified me against the less friendly looks from the minister's wife.

It seemed as if Susanna were being admonished for her remiss conduct towards the young señor Martinez, but that the doctor, who was sitting to one side, took up her defence.

I was standing in my old place again, and saw Susanna and Martinez dance the new circuit.

To begin with, her turned-up lip showed traces of that old, childish obstinacy after an admonishment; but later her expression became somehow more calm and thoughtful.

As I stood submersed in the sight of her, and probably weak after those many alternating agitations, I was all at once aware of that heavy, uneasy feeling of anxiety and disaster, that as a rule attends my visions, coming over me.

I sought to get out of the hall, but the sight grasped me first.

I saw Susanna's face, as she danced with Martinez, white as that of a thrillingly beautiful corpse, and the green garland with the little white flowers hung in her hair like wet seaweed. It was as if water were running down off her.

The blood streamed to my heart; the hall now grew dark, now turned beneath sparks of thousands of lights around before my eyes with the dancing couples.

I would surely have fainted, down by the door, had the doctor not taken me by the arm and led me out into the chilly passage and thence into a small guest room, where he let me drink some water and rest on the bed.

When he returned a half-hour after my attack and saw that I had come to, he gently and amiably sat down by the bed near me and began in his ingenuous way to talk, as he put it, 'straightforwardly' with me.

He had, he said, as he contemplatively used a pair of snuffers to trim the snuff of the lamp — which, presumably in order to be able to observe me, he had removed from the console-mirror and was now sitting with in his hand — been monitoring me that evening ever since I entered the hall, and thought he understood that I had a fancy for the pretty Susanna L., but was jealous of the young señor Martinez. He had also heard a bird singing about this matter before.

It was a feeling which many young people would only have had good of and benefited by, but for me, with my mental disposition, exciting moods like that would only be pernicious to the highest degree; he had unfortunately, he added softly, had experience of this with my own poor mother: her discovering, during my childhood, that her mental illness had been passed down to me, had only been but the chance occasion of her losing her senses.

As a physician and friend he wished to say this to me now, whilst he considered there was still time for me not to let this feeling establish roots. And he wished to say this not just for my sake, but also for that of Susanna, whom he loved dearly and would thus relucantly see led into something which, seen in worldly terms, could only end in sorrow.

There was something else I should weigh up, he continued — after a rather long pause in which he seemed to contemplate parting with the words, but then firmly resolved to — and that was that nor did my unhappy, heritable disposition make it particularly responsible of me to think of marrying; it could, he intimated, with a gesture as if he were carrying out a decisive operation on the lamp, indeed be looked upon in the same way as if a leper married, without worrying that he was thereby transmitting his illness down to his children. I should however — here he rose and placed his hand consolingly on my shoulder — not take this thing too seriously. The bitter means, and this was unfortunately the truth here, are usually the best, and moreover, according to his serious, mature reflection the unembellished, true reality was the only means to health and salvation for my sick, dreaming nature.

After having held the light above me a moment again, he removed himself, with a serious nod; he must have realised that at that moment I was not in a condition to carry on any conversation or to answer him.

It was in all friendliness the deathblow to all of my dreams and illusions.

I felt the numbness of the blow, even although my inner comprehension still had not properly admitted it clearly to itself. My life's old premonition of unhappiness was now, at last, con-firmed. Susanna had indeed only been borrowed sunshine for me, which was to be extinguished when it came to reality.

Whilst I really saw, with my inner eye, more than thought this, and music drifted in indistinctly from the ballroom, I lay so calm, so calm, and gradually felt myself somehow die, with a dull pain, from all that was dear to me in the world. It was as if my body were stiffening with sorrow, and Susanna's face without any ray of life stood before me now as something natural; my love was after all a story that had died.

As I was still lying there in a dim, stiff doze, through which everything outside only appeared to me in a half-fog, the door opened and a lady stepped in. In front of the mirror she hastily mended a trampled tear in her ballgown with a paper of pins, but suddenly stopped, alarmed at seeing someone lying on the bed, across in the half dark.

I recognised Susanna, and, as it seemed, an inkling told her too that it might be me, for she approached rather uncertainly and whispered my name.

She probably thought I was sleeping, since there was no answer, and that it was neither right nor time to wake me. For a moment she stood still right beside me, as if she were contemplating what to do, then she bowed over me until I felt her warm breath, pressed a soft kiss on my brow, and left.

A Christmas visit tends to last a couple of days, usually more, in those northern regions. This time it turned out that our party, because of my father's and the Martinez' pressure of work, was to travel the seven miles home in the dark the very next evening, whilst on the contrary most people were to wait until the following day.

The minister's family, however, were to remain there as guests together with the 'dignitaries' for the rest of the week, until Saturday.

In the meantime, the minister and his wife were to go out to visit a family in the vicinity the very next day. Susanna was allowed to remain behind.

I had, like the other guests, lain in until late in the forenoon; but in that time Dr K.'s words, that my position was like that of a a leper, had throbbed in my head like an abscess, steadily harder and more painfully, throughout all of my alternating conceptions, until their meaning all at once stood clear and unmistakably sharp before me.

For I loved Susanna a thousand times more than myself, and did I then selfishly wish to knit her fate to that of a man who was mentally ill, just because that person was me? And my mental condition might even deteriorate in the course of my life.

I began to feel that I was attaining sacrifice through pious courage, and thereby gained a beneficial, clear calm over myself. Moreover it was, of course, all in all no more than the best that I knew, namely to sacrifice my life for Susanna, and this observation in the end nearly gave me a fanatical desire to do so.

My decision was in any case taken, and my plan the simple one of talking straightforwardly, decisively and clearly with her, for I did not wish for all the world to fool her in any way.

It was that afternoon in the twilight, whilst the others were out taking walks, that I had the opportunity to talk to her.

That day Susanna was wearing her black silk confirmation dress, which suited her waist so well, the lace collar and narrow sleeves with cuffs above her wrists. Her hair was held up with a silver pin as at the ball, but otherwise without any embellishment.

Now she was sitting and thoughtfully listening to me, in front of the recently-fed tiled stove by which we had both sat down. Every time she bowed forward into the illumination from the mouth of the stove the glow fell on her expression-laden face, as, in striving to be truthful, I told her, possibly even in exaggerated colours, all about my mental condition and what Doctor K. had said about it.

As I was speaking I saw her face grow steadily more sombre and pale, until at last, with her elbows propped on her knees, she covered her eyes with her hands, so I could only see that her lips were trembling and that she was weeping.

When I came to what the doctor had said about my position being like that of a leper and that God Himself had thus placed an obstacle to our union, simultaneously trying, consolingly, to show her that we had after all — basically for all our lives, with the exception of the last couple of years — loved one another rather like brother and sister, she suddenly raised her head in wild vehemence so that I looked right into that tear-stained face, threw her arms around my neck, and thus constrained me to go down on my knees before her.

She forcefully pressed my head up to her pounding breast, as if she wished to protect me from everyone who wished to cause me harm.

Then she stroked the hair from my brow with her hand — I sensed her tears falling down onto my face — and affectionately repeated again and again, as if in a delirium, the words that nobody in the world would ever manage to take me from her.

This was too much for my weary, tormented nature; I grasped both of her hands and wept over them with my head in her lap.

My weeping grew steadily more vehement, until it eventually rose to a despairing, convulsive sobbing which I could no longer master, and which also quite alarmed Susanna; for she hushed me, called me by name, and in between kissed me like a child in order to quieten me.

I had such a deep need to weep right out that it could no longer be halted.

When I eventually grew calmer she again folded her hands about my neck, as if she thereby wished to focus my attention, bowed forward and looked long into my eyes with an expression in her troubled, pretty face at once so persuasively intense and so strong-willed.

I must, she eventually reassured me, with that toss of her head with which she always made her remarks penetrating, believe her that where it concerned us she knew a thousand times better what it was that God wished than any doctor, and that here we should both heed only God, not any doctor's worldly wisdom. I was, indeed, so often so monstrously simple that anyone could put words into my mouth about anything.

Such people as the doctor, she said, had no understanding of what love was. Had I been healthy and happy then it would clearly have been God's will that she was to share what was good with me, and thus it must surely equally be His will that it fell to that same love to share my sorrow and illness; but it was here that Doctor K. — she obviously felt a stronger and stronger hate for him the more she considered him — thought differently than the Lord. She believed, moreover, so surely — and her voice grew gentle and soft here, nearly whispering — that precisely our loving one another so much would be a better cure for my health than any doctor could find. In any case she felt for her own part that *she* would become ill in her mind, and despair, if I no longer loved her, for we had after all done that for as long as we each could remember, so that it was anyway too late to think of separating us.

One thing was to be firmly resolved now — at the thought her face acquired a trait of indomitable will which reminded me of her father — and that was that she would, as soon as possible, confide in her father everything about our relationship. It should no longer be any secret, both for my and for her sake. Her father loved her so much, and in case of need she would tell him seriously that it would be to no avail, either for him or any other — she meant with this her mother — to try any longer to have any doctor dupe me from her.

Some sort of 'brother- and sisterhood' between us, as she expressed it with scornful contempt in her look, she wished least of all to know of, and as if to have that thought properly crushed she bade me, as she stood upright before me and with passionate eagerness looked me in the face, give her my kiss as proof that we still were, and despite everything and everyone would always continue to be faithfully betrothed, even if I were never so healthy that we could ever marry here on Earth.

I embraced her, gave her my kiss warmly and passionately once, twice and thrice, until Susanna freed herself from me.

Whilst she was speaking it had occurred to me that, with her strong, healthy, loving nature she was fighting the fight for both of us, and for a right, which possibly could not be properly proved with words, but whose sanctity, I felt, lay outwith any artificial proof.

I had now regained Susanna in a different, truer and more real way than I had ever guessed or dreamed of, as I grasped that everything that could have been called chivalrous sacrifice on my part simply lay lower than our love, indeed was just a worthless infringement of it.

In true love the cross is borne by both of the lovers, and he who 'chivalrously' wishes to bear it alone simply cheats the other of a part of the best he has.

An hour after this meeting of mine with Susanna, which closed with renewed vows and pledges, I was sitting in the nearly dark winter's evening, whilst the moon sailed behind an infinity of small, grey clouds, in the stern of our five-boarder, together with my father and the two Martinezes.

Father sat, reticent, and steered, whilst the servants rowed against a fairly heavy headwind which was falling into the sound, in order that we could 'stretch out the sail' for the rest of the way.

In silence I thought over the great deal that had happened during this short visit, and felt so infinitely happy.

We reached home late that night. I tried to lie awake, thinking of Susanna and everything she had said to me, but slept like a log and awoke with a feeling of healthiness, happiness and joy which is only known by those to whose lot it has fallen to sleep the sleep of the truly happy.

And thus every night passed now. I fell asleep before I had finished my *Lord's Prayer*, sang in the mornings, and felt an almost abandoned lightness, joy and will to work the whole day.

What Susanna had said was confirmed: that our love would be a spring of health for me, better than any doctor's worldly sagacity was able to prescribe.

Chapter 10
The Storm

It was late in the afternoon of the Saturday after Epiphany that the terrible two-day-long storm blew up; it is still spoken of by many as one of the most hurricane-like that has passed across Lofoten in man's memory.

The storm worsened during the night; we could feel how at every blast of the storm the building would yield and its joints groan, and we were all sitting up by the light, waking, as if by some silent agreement.

Shutters, doors and crannies were painstakingly closed up. The rooftiles rattled noisily during the gusts of wind, so that we feared they might break the roof open, and in the blast the chimney-pots made a deep, eery, growling noise, which during the worst snatches at the building sounded like a high, terrible, giant's roar out in the night, sometimes almost like a wild cry for help.

We kept ourselves to the living-room, in a silence only now and again broken by some comment about the weather, or when one of the inmates came in from touring around the house to keep an eye on it.

My father sat in an uneasy dread for the sea-shed and for his *jægt*, which was lying down in the bay and which in the weighty sea, that came in despite the good position of the harbour, had been triply moored that afternoon.

Often I saw him folding his hands as if he were praying, and after that, somehow cheered up, walk back and forth across the floor for a while, until the dread again took him and he sat and looked, dark and pale, into the distance as before.

The storm grew worse rather than better.

Once we heard a dull boom that might well have been from the sea-shed. I saw the sweat pearl on my father's brow, and was seized by a deep pain at seeing his anxiety without being able to do so much as lift a finger to help.

A little later he took a light out to his office and returned with an old, large-print hymn book, in which he looked up a prayer, as well as a hymn to be sung at times of distress at sea.

Without having been called, everyone gathered in the living-room for a house service.

My father sat with the hymn book in those huge, callous hands, which he had folded in front of him on the table between the two lights.

First he read the prayer and then sang all the verses of the hymn through, whilst those of us who knew the tune gradually joined in at the refrains.

It was in all respects like the holding of a service at sea in a ship's cabin, whilst the vessel is in danger, and my father had probably got the idea from a scene like that in his arduous youth.

During the service it seemed to us all that the storm somehow abated, and that it only grew worse again once the service was over.

Of the elder Martinez it was reported that he was kneeling by his bed upstairs and uninterruptedly crossing himself before a crucifix. He had fewer grounds than we to be anxious, for his brig lay specially moored, by land in a little cove which lay sheltered from the weather and the sea swell. He now greatly regretted, however, that he had not gone on board to his son and his crew.

Towards morning it seemed that the weather eased a little, and tired though we were we went to bed, although a couple of the inmates stayed up.

Only when it grew light, at about ten o'clock that forenoon, could we survey the damage.

Several hundred tiles from the main building lay spread across the courtyard, part of the wall-panelling on the windward side was torn away, and the extreme end of the jetty lay askew down in the sea, since a couple of the piers supporting it had been battered by the sea swell. The sea-shed had also suffered some damage.

Our *jægt* was afloat, although obviously in danger. Two of its shore ropes had already snapped, for it had dragged its anchors, and everything now depended just on the third and longest rope, which was fastened to the mooring ring on the skerry out in the inlet of the bay.

Only the ship's dog was on board, a large, white poodle, with its forepaws on the bulwark aft, barking without our being able to hear the sound through the wind, whilst the sea swell washed over the bows of the *jægt*.

The situation was desperate, for the long shore rope hung as taut as a wire, the middle of it hardly touching the sea. Moreover, it was blowing so hard that a man could not easily stand upright, but had to creep along the windswept snow, so that there was no thought of help.

I had crept up onto a rise behind the house and was standing in the lee of a rocky crag, from where I could see both across the sea and down into the bay.

The West Fjord was lying, that winter's day, as if under a silver-grey smoke of scud, which was driving across the sea. In by land the waves ran like huge, green, foam-drifted hills, which were crushed against the coast with crashes of thunder, and with a monstrous undertow after them so that the shore would lie dry far out.

In one place, in a scar that dropped sharply down to the sea, every time a wave pounded in, a broad, monstrous jet of water would rise straight up and be driven by the wind like smoke, inwards and across the land. In another place the swell in a veritably titanic manner was storming a tilted stack, which now lay in foam, now was completely dry, and there I saw a poor, exhausted herring-gull that had presumably come out into the wind from its crag, fighting and tumbling in it, often with its wings turned almost inside out.

With dread my excited attention followed the *jægt* down in the bay.

To my surprise I saw a man on board it, and recognised the strong Jens Prentice, who had ventured there from the weather side in a six-oarer with one of our servants.

After a while on board he climbed, alone, with a line about his waist, down in to the six-oarer, and began the perilous task of hauling boat, against the sea-swell, along the taut shore rope out towards the skerry.

I waited, horrified, for the boat any instant to be filled, and it appeared to me that it shipped water several times. As the boat slowly managed to advance, father and all of our servants followed it tensely, down on the shore.

When Jens Prentice had reached the skerry, across which the waves were washing without cease, so that he often stood in water to his knees, he moored the boat and set about hauling in the line, and then after it he drew a thick hawser, which the man on board the *jægt* was gradually feeding out, towards him through the water.

He had just begun to belay it on the mooring ring and only had the last, conclusive couple of hitches of the rope left, when we all grew aware of three terrible wave-backs, that without a doubt would break over the skerry.

It was clearly a matter both of Jens Prentice's life and of the *jægt*, which with its one, overstretched shore rope would hardly withstand the pressure.

I saw French Martine, his sweetheart, wring her hands over her head and run out across the shore, almost as if she were thinking of throwing herself out into the water to him, and I do not believe that any of the others who saw this dared draw breath either.

It seemed that Jens Prentice had also noticed the danger himself; he hurried down into the boat, in which he could yet save himself, but it was only to fetch the line from it, which he calmly wrapped around his back a number of times and around the mooring ring, for he no longer relied upon his own giant's strength either.

He had hardly finished with this when the first wave, which he met with his head bowed towards it, broke white over him and the skerry. The time in between, before the second came, he used to make a new belay in the shore rope.

Again the wave came, and again Jens Prentice stood there unshaken, and now he succeeded in making the last hitch in the rope, which saved the *jægt*.

Now he had felt how a wave could press.

He threw the line from his back up over his round, huge shoulder, looked for a moment with that strong, pale face across at our buildings, as if it might well be that he was now bidding them farewell, and then bowed his head to the third and last wave, coming with its comb of spray above it, as usual greater and weightier than the preceding two.

When the wave had broken, churning, on the skerry there stood no Jens Prentice.

In my dread I had run down to the others. When I arrived, besides the boat, which had been severed from the skerry, the unconscious Jens Prentice had also been rescued, and was now being borne up to the house.

The wave had torn him with it, as the line which he had over his shoulder had slid up across his neck and taken skin and clothing with it. He now lay unconscious from the water and the pressure, and with one arm, which had been bloodily scraped by the line, in a distorted position; it was rubbed bare, in one place right to the bone.

Father, pale, supported him as they bore him and put him to bed.

When he awoke he spat a quantity of blood and it hurt him to speak; but father, who examined his chest, said happily that there was no mortal danger.

By this feat, in which he saved the *jægt*, Jens Prentice became a hero far and wide. In my father's house he became a trusted man from that day, and the next summer his wedding with French Martine took place.

Chapter 11
Conclusion

I can now calmly write down the little, to me so much, that remains to tell — for many years I would not have managed this.

The storm lasted from Saturday noon until Monday morning, when it gradually abated in the course of the morning to a complete calm in which, though, the sea still ran uneasy.

The same day, Monday noon, there landed at the manse landing place not the minister's white cabin boat, which was expected home, but an ordinary, tarred, farmer's five-boarder with many people in it.

Up from it to the house four of the men slowly bore between them a burden, whilst a large man and a little woman walked hand in hand, bowed, after them. It was a minister and his wife.

I understood instantly what had happened, and my heart screamed with despair in my breast.

The appalling tidings which soon afterwards reached us told me nothing new — they only confirmed that the person whom they had borne up was the minister's daughter, Susanna.

The minister's boat had only been a little over five miles away from their home that Saturday noon when the storm so suddenly came on. A 'down squall' had rushed from the mountain clefts into the sound with terrible might and had upturned the boat, which was not too far from land.

The minister had managed hastily to save his wife, up onto the hull, and his servants held on tight around the edge of the boat, as they drove before the wind the short stretch in to the beach. But he searched for his child in vain, where he might find and save her.

Whilst the water boiled around the boat, in desperation that strong man thrice let go in order to swim to where he imagined to himself he saw her in the water.

He wished to try again, but at his wife's wailing request his servants restrained him.

It was later said that they saw the damp sweat pearl down the minister's brow whilst he lay there beside the boat in the winter-cold sea, and that they believed it by no means impossible that for a while he thought of deliberately letting go and following his daughter.

Too late it was discovered that Susanna had been caught underneath the boat. A rope had wrapped itself around her so that she could not come up.

Her death had in any case been rapid and easy.

All of Saturday and Sunday, whilst the storm lasted, they had had to remain weather-bound in a farmstead in the vicinity, where the minister's wife had stayed in bed from exhaustion and sorrow.

The minister had as good as the whole time sat inside in the cold parlour where they had laid Susanna, and spoken with his God. For on Monday morning, when they were to travel home, he had a transfigured calm about him, had arranged everything, and throughout had consoled his poor, weeping wife.

I had lain in dumb, despairing sorrow that whole afternoon and that long night, and resolved to go across the following day to see Susanna for the last time.

Early that forenoon the minister unexpectedly stepped into our living-room and asked to speak to my father.

He looked pale and solemn as he sat on the sofa with his stick in front of him and waited.

When my father came through the door the minister stood up and with tears in his eyes took his hand.

After a pause, as if in which to compose himself, he evinced that my father here saw before him an unhappy but humble man, whom God had had to castigate strictly before his mind had really wished to bow to Him. He now wished, for the sake of his misfortune, to beg my father no longer to withhold from him his old friendship.

About the matter that was the cause of their distancing he did not wish to speak now; in it he had acted according to his best convictions. There was, however, something else that now lay on his heart, and here he laid his arm across my shoulder and drew me across to him confidentially, as he again sat down on the sofa.

His daughter Susanna, he continued, sighing at the name, had, a couple of days before God had taken her to Him, admitted him into her confidence and told him that she had loved me since she was small, and that we two had already given one another our betrothal vow, with the intention of telling our parents of our situation when I had become a student.

To begin with he had set himself against this on many grounds, amongst which first and foremost my sickliness and the youth of both of us. But Susanna had shown such a profound seriousness in this matter and expressed such an emphatic will that it had become clear to him, who knew her nature, that this love had been growing in her for many years and was now no longer to be plucked ut. And now it was his best consolation in the midst of his sorrow that, the same morning that they were to travel homewards on that ill-fortuned trip, he had given in and in addition promised her to endeavour to get my father to give his consent, too.

Instead he stood here now without any daughter, and only as one who related that the misfortune had also struck my father's house and touched his only child. He wished — he hoped with my father's permission — hereafter always to consider me as his son.

My father long sat surprised and pale; it was as if he took a long time to grasp what had been said.

Eventually he stood up and in silence gave the minister his hand.

Next he laid it on my shoulder, so that I felt its weight, looked me in the eye and said with a soft, strangely mild voice:

'The Lord be with you, my son! Sorrow has visited you young; do not be too frail to bear it!'

He wished to go out, in order to leave us alone, but changed his mind in the door and said that it was probably best if I now went with the minister and said my last farewell to Susanna.

A little later the minister and I were walking beside one another along the road. Our relationship had now become one of confidence, and he consolingly told me everything that Susanna had said in order to move him to consent.

'She knew, thank God,' he concluded with an easing sigh, 'that in her father she had a friend, in whom she dared confide in her hour of need.'

The minister led me into the living-room with its rolled-down blinds; he stood a moment at the bier, then the tears burst, running down that strong, broad face almost like hail, and he turned and left.

There she lay, maidenly in her white attire. They had twined a garland of green leaves with white flowers around her head, and I again saw for an instant the sight I had had at the ball. The delicate hands now lay piously folded across her breast, and with tears I recognised, on her betrothal finger, my own old bronze ring with the glass bead in it, which she had worn from the very moment that she had attained her father's consent.

That trait about her mouth, in life so expressive and energetic, was in death transformed to a quiet, happy smile, in which her beautiful, fine face with that broad, pure, marble brow shone, transfigured, like a saint's.

She lay so simply confident, as if she now knew the secret of the victory of faithful love over everything here on Earth, and she were going ahead in order to teach it to me with white wings on her shoulders, since God had not wished to allow that she should walk together with me down here, under my cross.

When I noticed that I ought to leave, in silence I recited my *Lord's Prayer* over her as a last farewell, impressed a light kiss on her brow, then on her mouth, and one on the folded hands, on the bronze ring, and left without looking back.

Two days later I followed Susanna to the Earth.

One sunshine day that winter, as I as usual was visiting the place where she rested in the churchyard, a snowdrift had driven about her grave. It lay pure and driving white, with the uppermost, fine edge like half-shone-through marble in the rays of the sun.

I took it to mean that Susanna wished to lead me to think of her in her shining bridal dress before God, to give me new courage to go my lonely way through life, and not fear that even that heaviest of all trials — madness itself, if it came and spell-bound me in its confusion — could separate us.

When I was to travel south with the steamer late that summer together with the minister and his wife, who had both in a short time grown visibly old and who had now sought a calling in a southern region, for the last time I went to take leave of my melancholy friend, the sacristan.

He again played for me that delightful, old, love-filled air which he had composed when he was twenty, and which I had thought suited Susanna and me so, but now also played the other part that belonged to it — it was strangely thrilling and sorrowful, but with consolation in it, like a hymn.

Here ends a poor, sick, Nordland boy's simple story; for the fact that, with my father's help, I became a student with *laud* — he died the same year that I passed my *Examen Artium*, as a respected but ruined man — and that I later became a mite literary, a tutor and alms-school teacher, is just to relate the external circumstances in a solitary life, that carries all its thoughts in what has passed.

My love for Susanna has, as she told me with such conviction, been the spring of health that has saved me from the utmost — madness.

When the unease would come across me and I would walk aimlessly around field and forest, it would always reach a point where I would see her in her white dress, floating past a short distance away — sometimes she would even mildly come towards me — and then the crisis would be over for that time.

In the last couple of years, as my illness has worsened, I have not managed to see her, and it has been burdensome, often as if the darkness were pressing hopelessly around me.

But now, as I lie here ill in my attic room, Susanna came one night when the full moon was shining, in her white bridal dress, with her garland and that rich hair, quietly smiling, across to the bed, and beckoned to me with the ring on her hand.

I know that she brought me the joyful tidings that I shall soon be able to go away and, up there, see her, my youth's beloved, again.

Glossary

Æsir [*Aserne*]: The chief gods of Norse mythology.

Alstadhaug: Church and place in Helgeland; church supposedly dating from the twelfth century.

Bjarmer: Old Norse name for the people living south and south-east of the White Sea.

Daily rowings: Fisherman's term: the crew received payment according to the number of days' fishing, and not the catch.

Draug: (pronounced *drowg*) In northern Norwegian folklore the spirit of a drowned man that sails at sea in a half-boat. A typical description is:

> Seers who travel on the sea often chance to see the draug. He is made like a man; but instead of a head he just has a clump, like the crown of a hat, covered in seaweed. His mouth and eyes he has in his chest. The draug is filled with evil and portends misfortune, and no-one likes to meet him.
>
> *(My translation)*

from: 'Draugen varsler Nils Jamtli', *Norske folkeeventyr og sagn*, O.T. Olsen, Kristiania, 1912.

Examen Artium: Norwegian school-leaving qualification of the time, allowing entrance to university.

Fetch [*Vardøger*]: In Norwegian folkore a kind of personal ghost that precedes one wherever one goes.

Fin: Until the 17th century, the word *Fin* was used in Norwegian to mean both Lapp and Finn; *Finn* remained a northern dialect word for Lapp (as opposed to *Finne*, Finn) until the last century. See also *Lapp*.

Fin Arnesen: (?—1065) Olaf the Holy's right-hand man.

Five-boarder [*Femböring*]: The flagship of the various Nordland boats; a square-rigged, open boat, usually about 12m (36ft) long, with rowing positions for five or six men. These boats looked remarkably like Viking boats, were very fast, although difficult to sail, and were the subject of numerous legends and tales.

Four-and-a-half-room five-boarder [*halvfemterums Femböring*]: A smaller version of the five-boarder, with four rowing spaces.

Haupt- und Staatsaction: Originally a form of theatre from seventeenth-century Germany; the term was used pejoratively to describe any low-quality theatre production.

Horseman [*Hestmannen*]: A well-known mountain in Helgeland, in the cliffs of which can be discerned a horse and rider.

Jægt: The most common cargo boat in northern Norway in the last century; single-masted, with a square-rigged sail, a cabin at the rear, and a 'loose deck'; used principally to carry fish from the North to Bergen.

Jumala: Originally the Finnish name for pagan gods, now used for the Christian God, too.

Kristiania: Now Oslo.

Kvæn: Originally an inhabitant of northern Finnland or of Norrbotten county in Sweden, later used to denote Finnish immigrants into Norway and their descendants, especially in Finnmark.

Lapp: This word is nowadays considered to be almost insulting, and the word *Sámi* is preferred and is the usual term today. I have kept Lie's usage, as the word 'Sámi' was not used at all when he was writing. The Sámi are an ethnically independent, nomadic people, and live throughout northern Scandinavia.

'Loose deck' [*'Flagedæk'*]: Deck on a ship, made entirely of loose boards to enable easy access to the holds and flexible carrying capacity.

Milk rings [*Mælkeringer*]: Northern Norwegian dish made of milk which is rapidly heated and then allowed to cool, originally in annular wooden bowls; it has a consistency like that of yoghurt, and is sour.

Phantasiestück [*Fantasistykke*]: Probably a reference to Schumann's *Phantasiestücke* for piano of 1838 and 1852; these are typical 19th-century Romantic mood pieces, based on a belief that extreme emotions not only could be evoked by but also portrayed by music.

St Olaf: King Olaf the Holy, christianiser of northern Norway.

Sea-draug [*Havdraug*]: See *Draug*.

Sea-man [*Havmannen*]: In northern Norwegian folklore a man on horseback who lived under the sea, and who would lure people after him.

Sea-shed [*Sjøbod*]: A warehouse built on a jetty or beside a landing-place; typical of any coastal settlement.

Siren folk [*Huldrefolk*]: In Norwegian folklore wicked, alluring sirens inhabiting hills and mountains; they are beautiful in appearance but have long, cow-like tails.

Snehætten: Mountain in the Dovre range, 2286m (7500ft) high.

Spectre [*Fylgje*]: In northern Norwegian folklore one's ghost or 'shadow' that follows one everywhere.

Storting: The Norwegian parliament.

Underground folk [*underjordiske*]: In Norwegian folkore leprechaun-like half-people that live underground and often cause misfortune or accidents.

Other
Stories

Translated by Brian Morton

Translator's Note

The stories Jonas Lie published in 1891 and 1982 as *Trold* and *Trold: ny samling* are written in a straightforward epical style, markedly simpler than *The Seer* or the work of his middle years. I have tried to keep this in mind while translating them. I have kept to much the same selection as R. Nisbet Bain's 1894 *Weird Tales from Northern Seas*, the only existing English translations that I am aware of, but I have avoided both Bain's addition to 'swain' and 'quoth' and his tendency to leave terms untranslated where there is no convenient English equivalent, such as *'femboring'* or *'sexæring'* for a five- or six-oared boat. Where they don't seem crucial to the narrative, or to any symbolic intention, I have ignored crewing figures. More problematically, perhaps, I have preferred 'Sea-Ghost' to *'Draug'*, 'Elf-Trout' for *'Huldrefiske'*, and the purely descriptive 'Wind-Seller' for *'Gan-Finn'*; these seem to me to be forgivable liberties, as do those changes where Lie's narrative transitions and identifications are not entirely clear.

The standard edition of Lie is P. Bergh's ten-volume *Samlede Dikter-verker* (1920–21) and the standard biographical accounts E. Lie's *Jonas Lie* (1933) and C.O. Bergstrom's *Jonas Lies vag til Gilje* (1949). The most useful English language accounts are the relevant chapters of Alrik Gustafson's *Six Scandinavian Novelists* (1940) and James W. McFarlane's *Ibsen and the Temper of Norwegian Literature* (1960).

Because they introduced me to Lie's work, thanks are due first to Robert and Louise Barnard, my hosts in Norway; to Gerd Bjørhovde, Frederik Christian Brøgger, Kjell Madsen and Øystein Aspaas, and to my students at the University of Tromsø; to James McFarlane and Janet (Mawby) Garton of the University of East Anglia; to the Reading Room staff of the British Library; and to Brenda Walker of Forest Books, for her patience.

These stories are dedicated to Pam, with all my love.

B.M.

Jack of Sjøholm

Back in the days of our grandfathers, folk bought good winds by the sackful from the Wind-Seller. The boats up in Nordland were puny things and the winter seas a death trap. In those days, a fisherman rarely died in his bed and only womenfolk and children were buried on dry land.

One winter a boat put out from Thjöttö in Helgeland and plied its way up through the East Lofotens. They trailed their lines for weeks on end, but the fish were not biting and there was nothing for it but to go home empty.

Jack of Sjøholm was with them and laughed at their lack of stomach. 'If there are no fish here they must have gone further north', he said. 'Come on, we didn't come all this way just for the good of our health.'

Jack was a youngster and it was his first trip but there was some truth in what he said and so the tillerman set their course northwards.

The next fishing bank was no better but they kept at it until the food and the last of their patience began to run out. Even now, Jack didn't want to turn back. 'We've got to go still further north. If we've come this far, we can go some more.'

They plied on, right up into Finnmark waters. There, the seas turned stormy and, with no hope of shelter under a headland, they had to make for open water and an even worse plight. Time and again, the bow nosed into green water, unable to ride the waves. The short day was already over when the boat turned turtle.

They clung to the keel and complained bitterly that it was Jack who had brought them to this pass. What of the women and families they'd left behind? Who'd look out for them now?

As the darkness deepened, one by one their hands grew numb and feeble and they slipped off into the water. Jack saw them all go, and the last sound he heard from each was a curse on his name.

He clung on, his knees tight round the keel. Anything was better than the freezing water. His mind was as numb as his hands and feet but in the dark he fancied he caught the echo of the drowning men cursing him.

He drifted for hours, till the sky showed the faint grey of a winter dawn. Suddenly the boat was pulled round by a strong on-shore current and Jack found himself beached, mid-way between white snow and black sea. In the distance, at the foot of a cliff he saw the smoke of a little hut, built in the manner of the Northern Finns. He managed to stagger to the door.

The Finn was as old as the landscape and almost as still. He sat in a heap of warm ashes, muttering into a sack before him, oblivious to Jack. All through the hut, there was a soft humming, like bees in midsummer.

The old man was alone, but for the young girl left behind to keep the fire burning and the pot stirred. Her father and brothers were off at the deer-fold.

Jack got himself dry and the Finn girl, Seimke, spoilt him with reindeer meat and milk. Half dead with tiredness, he lay down on a pile of silver fox skins. As he dozed, the room turned strange. The old Finn shuffled to his doorway and talked to the reindeer that were miles away. He scolded away the wolf and the bear, chasing them with spells. Then he opened up his wind sack and set a howling air round the hut, whirling the ashes like snow. When all fell quiet again, bees buzzed out of his furs, echoing his voice.

Odd as it all was, Jack couldn't put the boat out of his mind. When he was rested, he went back down to the beach. The boat was stuck fast, but the sea was washing round the stern, so he pulled it up clear of even the largest breakers. Looking at it lying there, he wondered if folk really did intend such a boat for these waters. The prow was low and blunt, better for digging into waves than riding them, and the hull was as square as a blanket chest. A really seaworthy boat would have a higher prow and sleeker lines, to cut through the waves.

He'd plenty of time to think about it. In the evenings there was only the Finn girl to talk to. She had obviously fallen for him. She followed him, on her feet or with her eyes, wherever he went and looked panic-stricken if he went down to push at the boat. She knew only too well how desperate he was to be away.

While the old Finn sat in his ashes, mumbling, Seimke honeyed up to Jack, murmuring soft words, slipping her hands into his furs. She led him off into a smokey corner.

The Finn's head twisted right round on his shoulders. 'The smoke's in my eyes, boy. What is it you're clutching at there?'

'Quick', said the girl, 'say I'm a bird you caught in a snare', and he could feel her trembling against him.

Her voice was so soft, her lips so close, that it was like listening to his own mind. She told him the Finn was angry and had put a spell on the boat Jack wanted to build. If it were ever finished, he'd have no market for his winds. 'Be careful and watch out for the magic bees.'

Jack saw his danger clearly but, as before, refused to be disheartened. In the early dawn, while the Finn dozed on, he headed out for the beach. There was something unfamiliar about the lie of the land. The snow drifts got deeper with every step and the shoreline had vanished. Above him, the Northern Lights flashed and hissed across the sky as if it were still night.

Beach and boat were gone. He was lost. He had turned inland by mistake but when he turned round a thick sea fog came round him like smoke, blinding him. He staggered about all the short day to his wits' end. As darkness fell again, the snow seemed to deepen anew. Jack sat down in despair of his life. As he brooded, a pair of snow shoes glided towards him out of the fog and stopped in front of the rock where he sat.

'You found your way here, you may as well take us both back' he said and put them on. The snow shoes carried him off, over hill and gully, sometimes almost as if they were flying. Jack recognized places he had passed that day but not in any order that let him set his own course. Suddenly, the snow shoes stopped dead. They were back at the Finn's hut and Seimke was waiting for him by the door. 'I sent my snow shoes out to fetch you. The Finn has put a spell on the land. You'll never find your boat. Come inside, you're safe so long as you keep still.' She smuggled him off into the same smoky corner and left him some food.

When Jack awoke, he heard an odd sound, a buzzing and chanting. The Finn was sitting in his ashes, muttering and mumbling spells while Seimke knelt with her face to the floor and hands clasped as if praying. Jack knew that the Finn was still searching for him out admist the snow and the sea fog and that only Seimke kept the old man from finding him.

Before light he went out quietly, covered himself with snow and came back in, stamping his feet and shouting that he'd been out looking for bears. 'What a fog! I've been all over and I only found the hut again by luck.'

The Finn's skins buzzed madly. He'd sent the bees out searching and they'd come back drowsy, little knowing Jack was there all along. The old man laughed and mumbled. 'Bears? Ha! I've bound them fast in their caves and gummed up their eyes. This bear I'll shut in a corner with a sleeping-peg in front of him till spring. That will stop his dreams of new boats.' He made signs with his hands and sent out two huge bees that melted patches of snow beneath them as they flew off to bring pain and sickness to the lowlands. Their cruel mission was to strike down a young wife at Bodu with consumption.

Seimke begged him not to think of his boat again but Jack thought of nothing else and she saw it was no use wheadling any longer. He had made up his mind to be off. However, she made him promise to wait until the Finn headed back off to his home on Mt. Jokmok.

On the given day, the Finn rooted through his hut. Far away as they were, he took stock of his herds, listened to his grandson's talk of losses and warned them again to beware of wolves. Then he swallowed a potion and began to spin like a humming top until all the breath went out of him and he fell in an empty heap like a pile of skins. His spirit had flown off to Jokmok, where the magicians sit in a fog, whisper about secret things and initiate new disciples. Only the bees stopped behind, humming round the empty furs in a shimmering ring.

In the night, Jack was awakened by something pulling at him, as if from far away. There was a draught of cold air and then a voice whispering. The Finn was there over him, his skin loose and wrinkled like a reindeer's throat, his breath like smoke, muttering spells.

Jack struggled gamely and the Finn's face grew dim and his voice failed. But then the magicians at Jokmok worked their spells. Whenever Jack went to work on his boat, his hands would falter and his head buzzed. Try as he might, he despaired of ever seeing the boat of his dreams in the water. He was marooned for ever.

Then one summer night, Jack and Seimke sat together watching the fish and the sea-birds out on the sound. 'If only someone else could build me such a boat, sleek as a herring and fast as a tern, then I'd be off.'

'Can I steer you back to Thjöttö?' said a voice from the shore below. There was a man standing there in a skin cap, turned so as to hide his face. Down by the rocks, just where they'd been watching terns dive for fish, there lay a long and narrow boat with the high prow and narrow stem Jack had dreamed of; there wasn't even a knot in the planks of her.

'I'd be grateful' said Jack, which set Seimke off crying and hanging on his neck. She promised to give him the snow-shoes that would take him everywhere he chose. She'd teach him salmon knots and reindeer-calls. She even promised to steal for him the Finn's bone-stick which would lead him to buried money. 'You can be as rich as the Finn. Just don't leave me!'

When Jack had eyes only for the boat, she wrenched out handfuls of hair and bound his feet so that he had to cut his way free of her.

'If I stay here with you and leave that boat down there' — he pointed to the stranger's leek hull — 'to sail off without me, my old shipmates won't be the last to cling to the cleats of an upturned boat. Now, do I go with a kiss or without?' Seimke threw herself into his arms like a cat but when she saw she could do nothing she rushed off back to the Finn's hut, and Jack knew that she would call up the old man against him.

There was no time to lose before the way was barred. Jack stepped from the boulders into the boat. The tiller fell into his hand as if made for him. The mysterious figure hoisted the sail and off they flew. There had never been such a boat. Though the sea was calm, the bow cut through it in a rush of white water.

They hadn't gone very far when a strange whistling filled the air. The gulls screamed and headed for shore, while the waves ran up like a wall behind. The Finn had opened his wind-sack and sent a storm after Jack. 'A full sail for such weather'; the fellow who held the sheets didn't take them in an inch, even as the water boiled up white to the very clouds.

If they didn't reach open water, they were lost. There came a hideous laugh from port. As the boat heeled over in a fresh gale, the heavy figure amidships leant with it, his huge sea boots awash with foam. But they scudded on, battered by wind and blinding spray on out into the open sea. The waves were so tall that Jack couldn't tell if it was night or day, whether they were at the bottom of a trough or high on a crest. Even so, the boat shrugged the sea aside as if its hull were scaled like a fish and its planks as smooth as a tern's egg. Peer, as he might, Jack couldn't see where the planks ended and the water began. For all the world it looked as if he were sailing in half a boat, the rest of it sheered away by the waves.

With night came the sea fire. It glowed like hot coals and, as they sailed through it, there was a hideous whistling to windward like giant bellows. Jack could hear answering cries of agony from all the upturned boats they passed. Deathly pale faces gaped from their keels, lit by the deathly glare of the sea-fire.

There was a shocking jolt and he woke to a cry. 'You're at home Jack. Don't you recognize Thjöttö?' When he came round a little he found himself lying among the boulders by his very own boathouse. The tide was so high that the foam glistened among his potato shaws. He could scarcely keep his feet in the wind, so he sat down in the lee of the boathouse and began scratching out a rough plan of the phantom boat in the damp sand. Pretty soon sleep and tiredness caught up with him.

When it was light again, his sister brought his breakfast, as if it were the most ordinary thing in the world for him to lying there of a morning. He started to tell her of his voyage to Finnmark and his encounter with the Wind-Seller and his journey home in the phantom boat. But she only nodded and smiled and went on her way. He got the same treatment throughout the day from his brothers and his mother and he soon came to realise that they thought he was touched.

'Fine', thought Jack, 'let them think what they please'. And from then on he spent most of his time down at the old boathouse. If he was mad, he might just as well behave like a real madman. He made himself a bed of skins down there and took to sitting on the roof-tree during the day shouting to the world that he was sailing with the sea-ghost. He made a whistling noise with his teeth and hung on to the rafters with only his sheath knife for support, as if he were clinging to his keel again.

If folk came to look at him, he'd roll back his eyes to show the whites and howl. After a few days his family would come no nearer than to leave a basket of food for him by the door. Soon, only little Malfri, his sister, would come down to him. She would sit and laugh at the toys he whittled and talk to him about the day they'd sail off in a boat like a bird, such as no one had ever sailed in.

If a stranger chanced on him without warning or tried to spy on what he was doing, he'd clamber up into the rafters and bang about till they went off, more puzzled than ever. Sometimes they'd come stealing back again when they heard him laugh and laugh, but mostly folk left him to himself.

He worked best at night or when the wind ripped at the roof-turves and the sea-wrack plastered itself against his door. It was on such nights, while the wind whined and hissed through the stones of the walls, that the outline of the phantom boat was sharpest in his mind. The winter days were short and the lamplight cast huge shadows. Jack slept only during the short day, where he fell, pillowed on the wood-shavings from his night's work.

He took great pains. If there was a plank which wouldn't sit true, even by a fraction, he'd take out all its neighbours and do them again.

By Christmas he was nearly finished, with just the upperworks to smooth off. By now he was working so hard that he'd lost all track of time. His plane was curling big pale shavings off a plank when he spotted a dark shadow edging along the wood. It was a huge and hideous bee nosing at the planks and boards with its blunt face. When it reached the keel it whirled its wings and rose up into the darkness.

Jack's heart sank like a stone and doubt came upon him. The creature hadn't come looking for nectar to be sure! He took up his lamp and his biggest mallet and began to go over every inch of his craft, testing every plank and nail, no longer able to believe in what he had done. The shape and lines suddenly looked out of true. The prow was too tall and the line round the gunwale was kinked as if two different boats had been awkwardly nailed together. As he looked on in despair, his scalp icy with sweat, his lamp went out.

He grabbed up his mallet again and leapt out through the boathouse door. Grabbing a cowbell, he began to swing it about him in the darkness. 'Is that me you're ringing for, Jack?' came a voice, and there was a sound behind him like surf sucking back over shingle. He turned back into the boathouse and there on the keel-bone sat a figure in a wet grey sea-jacket, with a cap pulled down over its face. It was the Sea-Ghost himself.

Jack snatched up a baler and flung it at the figure but it passed through like smoke and clattered on the wall behind bouncing back inches past Jack's spinning head.

The figure did nothing but blink its eyes below the cap's peak. Jack spat at the evil thing but the gob just flew back in his face. 'Yours, I think' laughed the voice. But suddenly the night opened and Jack seemed to see before him a thriving boat-yard. Out on the water, there lay a beautiful eight-oared fisher, so lithe and shapely that he could not take his eyes off it. The Sea-Ghost blinked his glowing eyes. 'I brought you back home and now I'll put some good work your way. But you'll owe me a little tax on it. Every seventh boat you finish, you must call on me to put in the keel-board.'

Jack felt ready to choke and saw perdition opening up at his feet. 'You surely don't expect to get the secret out of me for nothing' said the Sea-Ghost. 'If you want a sailing boat, the price is a drowning boat. One in seven; that's the bargain. Knock three times on your keel-plate and you shall build boats the like of which were never dreamed of in Nordland.'

Twice during that long night, Jack raised his mallet above the hull, only to put it down again. The vision of that sleek boat would not leave his mind alone. He could almost smell the fresh tar and feel the ropes and lines in his hands.

Once, twice, three times, his mallet fell with a thump on the keel.

That was the laying of the first boat at Sjøholm. In the autumn folk gathered on the headland to watch Jack and his brothers put out.

As they jostled like puffins on the shore, the boat cut a foaming wake through the riptides, ducking like a gull past the skerries and headlands. As it passed fishing boats, men dropped their lines and pots to watch it pass, open-mouthed.

Next year's boat was only faster and lighter and from then on every year saw one better and faster. Until the seventh. It was to be the largest and fleetest of all. Jack paced up and down in his yard, wondering what to do. When he came down to work each morning, the boat seemed even more beautiful than it had the night before. It was the talk of the place.

The Sheriff of Helgeland in those days was a harsh man, who laid heavy taxes on the fisherfolk, taking more than his rightful share of fish and eider-down and grain. His henchmen showed no mercy and it was they who brought back to him rumours of a wonderous new boat, soon to be made ready for the water. In his youth, the Sheriff had been a fisherman himself and he coveted the boat. He came down on Jack at Sjøholm like a hawk out of a clear sky. 'It seems to me that you haven't been paying your taxes young man. I'm fining you a half mark of silver for every boat you've built. By right', he said working himself up into a fine fury, 'you should be carted off to the prison at Skraar and clapped in chains in the darkest corner'.

But the Sheriff knew what he was about. After looking around the almost finished new boat, carefully hiding his lust for it, he decided that he could be merciful as well as just. 'I'll take the boat in lieu of your fine and sentence.'

Jack took off his cap and bowed humbly. 'There's nobody I'd rather see at the tiller of this boat than Your Worship.'

When the Sheriff sailed off, Jack's mother and brothers and Malfri stood crying by the quayside for the loss of it. All Jack did was stand on the roof-tree of his old boathouse and laugh fit to burst.

Late in the autumn, the news came back that the Sheriff and his eight crewmen had gone down with the boat over in the West Fjord.

Jack's business grew apace. It wasn't possible to build a tenth of the boats people wanted and it became a special favour if he were to take on your order. As the boat slips filled up and emptied, Jack quickly lost count. If a boat he had built went down to the fish every now and then, he still had his money in his pocket. Someone else's misfortune, it was.

As silver dollars began to line up on his counting desk, Jack became a power in the place, not at all the kind of man that people like to cross. His business touched lives all over Sjøholm.

One Sunday his brothers and Malfri went off to church in one of Jack's boats. Jack was working on a new boat and when his head boatman came in to say that evening had come, a wind was brewing and they still weren't back, he chased him angrily and went back to his plans. 'Are you saying you think one of my boats isn't safe? Is that it?' The boatman went on his way.

But that night, Jack couldn't find sleep. The wind whistled outside and plucked at his walls. There were distant cries out on the water. And then there came a knocking at his door and someone calling him by his name. 'Get back to where you came from', Jack cried huddling beneath his covers. 'Can't you leave me in peace of a night, or am I going to have to build me a thicker door?'

The knocking went on and Jack could hear a wet swishing on the doorstep and the rattle of fingers on the latch. Jack only laughed now. 'The boats built here don't go down before the first puff of breeze', he said.

But the door suddenly burst open and there stood little Malfri and her mother and brothers, all dripping with sea-fire. Their faces were blue and pinched with the death agony. Malfri's arm hung broken and bleeding around her mother's neck, where she had clutched her as she went down. Reaching out toward Jack with the other, she begged for her life back.

Jack now knew what had befallen them. He put out into the dark waters to search for them, rousing up as many of his neighbours as he had boats. They searched in vain all night. Towards morning the boat came back of its own accord, upside down and with a huge hole stove in the keel. Jack knew at once whose work this was and from that night on he changed. In the daytime, so long as he could hear the hammers and saws, he was fine and boats still slipped from his yard like seals from a rock. But no sooner than his workmen had gone home of an evening than he began to hear his mother banging about in the darkened kitchen, little Malfri skipping down empty passageways and his brothers clumping their way up to bed. There was not a sight of any of them, but watches of glowing damp on the floorboards. Sleep deserted Jack. As Malfri whispered at his lock, he would lie and tot up how many drowning boats he'd sent off to sea. The numbers crept up with every count.

He took to going down to the yard at midnight, testing keel-boards with his mallet to see if he could somehow tell which ones were sevenths. But they all sounded alike, strong and supple, the wood beneath the tar clean and fresh.

One night he couldn't get a new six-manner out of his sleepless head, so he went down to the bridge where it lay ready to put out and banged at its keel-boards. As he bent to his task, there was a strange belching sound out to sea and a sudden stink of rot. Next he heard a wading sound and as he looked up saw groups of people coming ashore, men, women and children. They walked stiffly and crookedly, and passed clean through whatever obstacle lay in their path, coughing and creaking. Crew after crew, in fives and sixes and eights, marched along the headland path and in the moonlight Jack could see their bones glowing. Their eye sockets stared and their teeth dripped water. Soon the place was shoaling with them and Jack realised that these were the very folk he had tried to tally in his bed.

Jack rose up in the prow of the boat. 'If it hadn't been for me and my boats, there would have been more of you yet', he cried, but they continued to come at him like sleet, staring blankly and gnashing out each one his tale of woe.

To save himself, Jack set sail from Sjøholm, but no sooner was he beyond the bar than his sheets went slack and he lay becalmed. Out beyond him in dead water was a great mass of rotting planks, all tangled together, burst open and slimy green, with none of the sleekness he'd given them at his yard. Dead hands gripped at the boards with white knuckles, constantly slipping back into the water.

Jack called on all his seamanship to get away, tacking and luffing on the slightest breaths of air. He looked behind him to see if the nightmares were following, but now the water was a tangle of dead fingers and gaffs bit at his stern-boards.

There was a sudden gust of wind and the boat began to drive along among white rollers. The sky darkened and a thick sleet came down as the flotsam around greened and stank. He set his course by rocks which turned out to be cormorants. They came back at night to taunt him, flitting about his mast.

At last the sky began to clear a little but the air was now alive with humming bees. The sun burned down on a snowy shore and he began to recognize the place. The smoke was from the Wind-Seller's hut on top of its snow-hill and there were the old Finn, stretching up the skin of his scalp in welcome, as if it were a cap and Seimke by his side.

In the sunlight she looked old and bent as she spread reindeer skins, but the look she gave Jack was like a cat's as she jumped up, shading her eyes with her hand.

Jack felt a strange longing come upon him and he put ashore.

He stood beside her and she threw her arms around his neck and laughed and fondled him and wouldn't let him go, drawing him back into the hut.

In the ashes, the Finn shifted angrily, muttering to his bees, to keep between Jack and the door. Since Jack had begun his business there was no more trade in winds and the Finn was quite ruined, reduced to a beggar. From all his herds, he was left with but one doe.

Seimke crept behind Jack again and whispered in his ear that he must bid for the doe. She put the reindeer skin around her and stood over in the smoke so the Finn could only see the grey pelt. Jack felt at her legs and haunches, then began to bid. The old man nodded and spat, but wouldn't take Jack's price. Jack raised and raised his bid as the Finn grew angrier, whipping up his ashes into a blizzard and setting his bees angrily buzzing among his furs.

Jack raised his bid again and again until the total reached a whole seven bushels of silver. The Finn laughed till his skin shook. 'A bargain.'

Jack lifted Seimke up and rushed down with her to the boat, holding the reindeer skin up behind him to fool the half blind old man. They headed out to sea and Seimke clapped her hands with delight.

The Northern Lights shot across the sky and all the colours there are played across her upturned face as she talked and tongued spells at them.

When it grew fully dark, she lay with her head on Jack's chest, with her warm breath at his chin. Her black hair spread over his mouth and under his hands her heart throbbed like a bird's. He spread the reindeer skin over her and the boat rocked them back and forth on the heavy swell, like two children in a cradle. They sailed on for a night and a day. They sailed on until the land and the skerries and sea-birds were left far behind.

It's Me

All they ever talked about was what an easy life they'd have if they lived in the valley. When Gygra's daughter thought how much she longed to be some rich man's servant girl, she'd sink into a sulk, stomp her feet and kick sparks off the boulders.

'If you're so hell-bent on the easy life', the others said to her, 'get yourself off to the troll's and have that nose rubbed down a bit. Tidy yourself up and put a comb in your hair instead of that old rake.'

Gygra's daughter marched up the middle of the river, under the falls and into the ground-gnome's cave. Scrubbed and combed and knocked into shape, she was ready for the valley.

One evening in summer a big, raw-boned girl strode into the merchant's kitchen and asked to be taken into service.

'Can you cook?', the merchant's wife wanted to know. The girl looked a strapping corn-fed wench who'd make no bones about a bit of extra yard-work if the need ever arose. They took her on gladly.

She wasn't exactly dainty in her ways. The first day, when she was carting in a load of wood, she pushed against the door so roughly that she bust its hinges. The merchant soon gave up mending it, for no matter how many times he strengthened the nails, she managed to loosen them the very next time she went out for logs.

She didn't seem to understand washing up either and the pans and plates piled up from one week's end to the next, until they overflowed the kitchen shelves. It wasn't so very much better when she did set to with her scouring brush. Pans bent out of shape in her grip, plates splintered at a look. When her mistress showed her how it should be done, she just gaped and pretty soon the

111

kitchen looked like a skittle stall at the fair. One thing she was good at was eating, that and warming her smelly clothes by the fire. She was putting away as much food as all the other servants together. Behind her back, they called her Nosebag.

So husband and wife decided they would be well rid of her and the merchant went off to give her a last dressing down. He found her sprawling over the kitchen table doing nothing but gawping out of the window at the merchant's boats waiting to be relieved of their cargos of oil. He lost his temper. 'Be off with you this very day, and good riddance!'

Nosebag only showed her teeth in a grin and said she'd show him that all that good bread hadn't gone to waste.

She lumbered down to the waiting boats, snorted once back at him and, to everyone's amazement, hefted a full barrel of oil up onto her back. She carted it back up the path to the house, barged into the kitchen and asked the merchant politely to tell her where he'd like it put.

He only stood with his mouth hanging open, so back she went and barrel after barrel came up the path the same way until the kitchen was stacked to the rafters. The merchant roared with delight and slapped at his belly for breath. This made all the difference to things. Back he went to his wife. 'What a marvellous girl this is', he said.

For all his compliments, though, Nosebag wouldn't lift a finger in the kitchen from that day onward and the family were reduced to warming up whatever was left in the larder. Nothing would prise her away from the fireside.

When the mistress complained anew, the merchant said they shouldn't expect too much of a youngster. 'Growing girls need their rest. She's tired from all that lifting.'

Nosebag would only stir herself for the merchant. She jumped up with a grin whwnever he came in and was always ready to go off on errands for him, taking the bucket to the well, or going to the corn store for a sack of meal. So long as the mistress was out of the way she treated the house as her own.

She'd hang the porridge pot over the fire, bring out a huge bowl of treacle and set herself down to eat her fill. If any of the servants asked for a share, she'd only answer 'Nay, tis mine!'

They were afraid of her. Since the day she'd unloaded the oil, they knew she had the master on her side.

The mistress, though, kept a watch on the treacle pot and checked on the hams and gingerbread. Whenever, she came into the kitchen, there Nosebag would be and always licking her fingers. She was getting fatter by the day.

Eventually the mistress took away and hid the larder key. Nosebag redoubled her niceness to the merchant, forever looking out for things — preferably food — that needed to be carried up and put in store. It didn't matter how big: barrels of fish, casks of sugar, sacks of meal. Watching her, the merchant laughed in delight. 'There's not one of my men can carry a load like that!'

When he came home from his first selling trip of the winter, it was Nosebag who ran to meet him at the quay, take off his dripping oilskin and loosen his sea-boots. He was cold and shivering, so she wrung out his socks and put him in the warmest corner of the fireplace. When his wife came in with a mulled ale for him, she was annoyed to see the girl fussing around her man and stamped off in a rage.

First thing in the morning the merchant was up shouting for fresh socks and wet weather gear. He was bad-tempered at the thought of going back out in such filthy weather. He wrenched open the kitchen door and was just about ready to ask peevishly how much longer he was going to be kept waiting when his mouth fell open in amazement and delight. All his gear was hung out ready for him, snug and dry; his souwester and jacket, his jersey and his trousers. In the middle of the floor stood his boots, shining with dubbin and greased in every strap and corner. 'You couldn't get another such girl for love or money.'

This was the last straw. His wife stuck the jacket in his face, so he could smell the burning. The whole side of it was melted with heat. Then she dragged out the butter barrel and showed him the bootprints in the middle of it where the girl had tried to grease his boots.

The merchant was quite crestfallen at this. His face crumpled and he began to cry. 'You don't understand. What if she did use best butter for my boots. She meant well and I'll not be the one to put her out of this house.'

His wife gave up and let Nosebag rule the kitchen at her whim. Before long she had taken up residence in the larder and if anyone rattled at the latch and called out 'Who's that?', she'd just answer 'It's me.'

113

She squatted on the gingerbread box and ate and ate. The merchant only encouraged her, asking gently if she was getting enough. 'We don't want you to starve, do we?'

Towards Christmas, people were getting ready for the fishing. The merchant's wife was bustling about readying things for the fishermen. She got down the cauldron and organised the pickling barrels. She brought in bakers to make waffles and pancakes. With all the activity, it seemed to Nosebag that she'd never know another moment's peace. The larder door was banging like a drum from morning to night.

After a couple of days, Nosebag decided to put an end to all the nonsense. She got out the soft soap and smeared it all over the pantry passage and threshold. When the mistress came bustling through the next morning carrying a butter churn and bowl, she slipped and fell down the stairs, where she lay until Nosebag found her and scooped her up. She carried her in to the merchant crying and yelling fit to burst. 'Poor madam, such a pother and guddle, and now she's broke her leg.' Everyone was crying, but the merchant hardest of all. 'You're worth more to us than we'll ever count', he said to the girl.

Nosebag was now in charge, in the stores and in the house. She shooed all the hired cooks and bakers away. They were eating the master out of house and home, she said! She packed up the sailor's boxes — with fat instead of butter and no treacle for their waffles! — and the merchant had never known the fishing better or more quickly organized. He was amazed when Nosebag took him up to the stores and showed him how little had been used. 'With mother bed-ridden, you're the boss', he said. For Christmas, Nosebag baked and roasted and stewed but kept the servants and workers to such a narrow diet that they were chewing spoons and biting at old bones to silence their rumbles.

Upstairs, there had never been a better Christmas, with veal and ham, cakes and pancakes. The guests were delighted. So the merchant took her by the arm and led her off down to the shop and showed her where she might pick whatever her heart desired, dresses and kerchiefs and beads and silks, all of them worthy of his own dear wife. He left her there and went home.

Later that evening, he and the bailiff and the sexton were playing cards in the parlour. When Nosebag came in their jaws dropped, for she had decked herself out like a shire horse at a show, with ribbons knotted in her hair and kerchiefs draped all about her. When the merchant didn't join the others' laughter they decided to agree that she looked absolutely charming.

They had cause to see her often that evening, for she plied them with cakes and brandy. After three successive nights of it, they were so addled that she picked them up like logs and tucked them into their beds. The celebrations went on long after Twelfth Night. Nosebag smiled and stared, but if ever she thought no-one was paying her enough attention, she would plant herself in the middle of the floor and bawl 'It's me, me!', showing off her finery as she spun round.

When it came time eventually to go, the guests agreed that there never was such a girl. When the fishermen opened their boxes out at sea, they weren't so sure. Things were a mite thinner since Nosebag took the reins. So much so that their food ran out just when the cod began biting in earnest. The merchant's crews had to abandon the shoals to the other boats.

When he saw them return almost empty and sit by his quay at the height of the season, he nearly burst a blood vessel. They weren't back an hour before they were up at the house to complain. Their food had been stale, they said, hardly fit for dogs let alone working men. The pancakes were like shoe leather, greased with rancid fat. The bacon was all rind and the cured mutton all bone.

The merchant stomped up to the store-room. Nosebag told him it was all he could manage to meet the costs of the lines and hooks and baskets, without having to spoil them all with cakes and butter and bacon. 'How can them starve, with all them fish about?' she asked.

And she handed him a waffle to taste, filled with butter and treacle. He'd never had one as good or as rich, so he went back down with the butter and syrup still dripping off his chin, to give them a piece of his mind. He kicked them all out, sacking old Thore, who'd been his tillerman for years and his father's before that.

Only Kjell the herdsman had kept out of the little delegation and hidden himself up on the threshing floor. As he watched the master gobbling like an angry turkey in the yard below, he spotted the mistress hobbling to her bedroom window and staring out. When she heard old Thore get his books, she began to take on dreadfully, wringing her hands and crying. Even as she watched the old man shuffle off with his cap in his hands, she could not find the courage to call out after him, for there in the dooryard was Nosebag, a great basket of flourcakes in her hands.

Though Kjell felt like crying too, he vowed that Nosebag wasn't going to make herself any plumper under that roof. Or he'd know the reason why. He began to watch her at every turn and much of it made no sense at all.

Towards spring, when they put the mast on a new boat for the Bergen run, the merchant was so caught up in the excitement that he spent the day rushing back and forth between house and quay. The boat was the best he'd ever had and he decided that he should take Nosebag down the coast. 'She's never seen Bergen, poor lass, and mother's been there often enough.' Kjell smelt a rat in all this.

As soon as Nosebag heard of the trip she turned the place upside down and cleared the shelves of anything remotely wearable. At nightfall, with everyone else long since in bed, Kjell spotted her making her way over to the storehouse with a light. He jumped up and followed her, peering in through a crack in the door.

Inside, she was chopping up cakes and hams and salt beef and stuffing a sea chest with tit-bits for the voyage. the casket was so full that she had to sit on the lid to close it. Even then the lock wouldn't catch and she had to jump up and down on it, for all the world like an angry carthorse. When she was done, she carted the chest off to the wagon and smuggled it among the stuff there. That done, she went off to the stable and untethered the horse. All hell broke loose!

The horse could smell witchcraft and wouldn't allow himself to be put in traces. He bucked and shied and kicked until she lost her temper and kicked out at him with her back legs, the way a mare does, whinnying and snorting through her nose. Kjell had never seen the like and ran to fetch the merchant.

Out in the moonlight, the horse and Nosebag were lashing out at each other, plunging and rearing, striking sparks the pair of them from the flagstones of the yard. Their long legs flicked and flashed.

The merchant was dizzy with shock. Blood poured from his nose and Kjell had to help him to the horsetrough to duck his head in cold water. That night the merchant didn't go to bed, but paced about and stamped his feet. In the morning he sent Kjell to fetch back old Thore, with a message that he should put on his holiday clothes and make ready to row madam out to the big yacht. She was going to Bergen after all. She would have a silk dress and a gold chain. Above all, they were going to find themselves a Bergen serving girl.

It was early morning when they hoisted the sail and made ready to set off. But they waited until Nosebag came down the path and onto the quay, puffing and snorting, with ribbons in her mane of hair, dragging the wagon behind her. When they weighed anchor, she was still waiting by the quay, prancing and tossing her head. The merchant stood on the deck with his pipe and his telescope. In the distance he could hear her calling 'Me! Me! Mee-ee-ee!' The longer he looked at her through his glass, the more she tossed and flounced. But then she spotted his wife standing by his side and realised that he was going away without her.

She kicked and smashed at the planks of the quay then dived into the sea and caught the anchor chain in her teeth, hauling at it till it broke, tumbling back in the shallows with her hooves in the air.

As they sailed away, the merchant laughed and brayed and shook till he nearly fell overboard.

In the Blue Mountains

The farmer's son was bound for Moen. He was to be the drummer at the yearly manoeuvres. Because his route went through the mountains, he could practise his rolls and his stick-work to his heart's content, without making people laugh and without the cloud of small boys who were attracted to him like flies.

Every time, though, that he passed a mountain steading, he'd beat out a call to the girls there. They'd come out and stare after him.

The summer was at its height. He'd been practising since dawn and was sick to death of it. He struggled up the slopes, his drum on his back, the sticks tucked into his belt. Out on the hills, the sun was baking but in the corries and gulleys there was the same cool you feel behind a waterfall. The hill was covered in blae-berries and he bent so often to stuff handfuls in his mouth that it took an age to reach the top.

On the downslope, the ferns were tall and the alders shady. He couldn't resist stopping for a rest. He put down his drum, bundled his tunic under his head and put his cap over his eyes. In no time, he was asleep.

As he dozed, he dreamt that someone was tickling his uncovered lips with a blade of grass; when he started awake he swore he could hear giggly laughter.

By this time, the shadows were getting longer and down below in the valley the evening mist was beginning to form scarves and ribbons.

As he shook out his tunic, he saw a coiled snake peering at him with tiny, cunning eyes. He threw a stone but all the snake did was catch its tail in its mouth and roll off like a hoop. And again, the sound of someone giggling.

It seemed to come from a stand of birch trees which was bathed in sunlight and spangled with water drops, which glistened so brightly that he was dazzled.

He could barely make out what was moving amid the trunks but he fancied that he glimpsed a slim girl, laughing and peeping at him from behind her hand, as dazzled as he was.

When, a moment later, a dark blue blouse appeared among the branches, he was after her like a flash. He had almost decided to give up the chase when a swirl of skirts and flash of bare shoulder spurred him on. Even so, he was beginning to wonder if it was nothing but heat and imagination. Then, again, he spotted her against the green, her braids tangled by the branches. She stopped and looked back at him, pretending to be frightened.

She was carrying his drumsticks! Determined now to catch her, he set off again, while she twisted and turned, laughing and mocking, her hair flickering in the light like a snake's tail.

At the crest, she stopped, cornered by a fence and turned, taunting him with the drumsticks. He was near enough to make a determined grab. As she flicked through the fence, he tumbled after her, and found himself in an enclosure looking up at a little farmstead.

'Randi, and Brandi, and Gyri and Gunna!' At her call, four girls came running out. The last of them had rosy cheeks and heavy chestnut hair. She stood by shyly as if embarrassed by her sister's pranks, uncertain what to do or say. She sidled nearer with downcast eyes and only when she was close by him did she lift her face. Her eyes were blue and wide, but had a chilly, cutting depth to them.

'Come along with me instead, and dance', said a black-haired girl 'or are you too tired?'. Her mocking breath was hot on him as she pulled at his arm, skipping and clapping her rump.

'Wait in line, Gyri, you crow', the others cried, still giggling. 'Go tie yourself up'. At their words, she let the boy go and staggered away, her hands twisting behind her as if caught. He stared at her as she fell quiet.

The girl he had chased, the prettiest of them all, turned to tease him again. 'Run as you like, you'd never catch me, and you'll never find your drumsticks either'. But no sooner had she spoken than she flung herself down and sobbed. Between her gasps, he could make out broken words 'I followed you all day, and I've never

119

heard such a drummer or seen a lad as handsome when he sleeps. It was me that kissed you'.

The shy girl beside him whispered 'Watch out for the snake's tongue. It kisses before it stings.' And as he looked back to the weeping girl on the ground, he remembered the snake on the hillside, how it darted and she ran, how her hair gleamed in coils, and how she looked up at him through her tears with cold, clever eyes.

Suddenly, a bent, awkward little figure popped up on his other side, smiling secretly as if she had much to tell him. The light was buried a long way inside her eyes and shadows stole across her face like afternoon fading over the hill.

'Come away with me and you'll hear such music as you never knew there was. I'll play for you things no-one else has ever heard. You'll hear the laughter in trees, the cry of roots, the songs of the mountains. And when you've heard that there's nothing more you'll ever want.'

But at her words there came a scornful laugh and the boy turned to see a tall girl with a gold braid on her brows. With powerful arms she lifted a massive horn, tossed back her head proudly and blew a note as solid as the rock on which she stood; the summer twilight echoed to it.

The pretty girl on the ground put her fingers in her ears and mimicked the sound as she laughed. Then she looked up, peering through her hair as she had hidden through the alder branches and whispered 'If you want me, you'll need to help me' — he wondered at the strength in her arms as he raised her — 'but you'll have to catch me first' and she darted off toward the house.

Suddenly, she stopped and stared straight into his eyes. 'Do you like me?' Close enough to kiss her back, he couldn't say no. 'The boy wants me', she called back in the direction of the house. 'This is for you to decide, father.' And she drew him on toward the door, where there sat a little bearded man in hodden clothes, with a cap perched on his head and little slitted golden eyes.

'I know what you're after', he said, nodding slyly. 'You want your stake out here in the west, your homestead in the Blue Mountains. That's it, isn't it? And welcome you are.'

'It's a fine offer' said the boy, understanding at last, 'but too sudden to decide. Down our way, the thing is to send out go-betweens, to see how the land lies first.'

'That's what you did, indeed', said the girl sharply, 'here they are.' And she held up his drumsticks.

'Then we like to have a look over ourselves. No reflection, but just to make sure.'

At that she grew green and small and there came a poisonous glitter in her eyes. 'Isn't that what you did. Didn't you chase me and court me down there, half the day, and didn't my father hear you?'

'I didn't have to chase so very hard', said the boy, fearful of the sting in this wooing. At his words she bent backwards in a perfect circle, then shot forward a glittering head, until the old man lifted his stick and she stood upright again with her hands bound to her flanks by her silver girdle. 'Are you one of those boys afraid of girls?' she laughed. 'Perhaps if you want me you might get run right off those legs of yours.' As she skipped and wheedled in front of him, her shadow looped and coiled on the grass.

They seemed hell-bent on him, but a soldier bound for man-oeuvres knows his duty. 'I came for my drumsticks, not to find a wife and I'll thank you for them back.'

'Don't be hasty, young fellow, have a look about you first.' As the old man pointed with his stick the trees parted and the drummer saw broad pastures dotted with cows. Their bells echoed the clatter of the prettiest milkmaid's buckets and coppers. There was wealth here, to be sure.

'Maybe my dowry isn't good enough for you. But we've four such farms in the Blue Mountains and the best of them is a dozen times as broad and rich as this.'

The drummer couldn't keep his mind from those coiling shadows and asked for a little time to consider. At this, the girl began to sob anew and accused him of leading on an innocent girl, fit to drive her mad. 'I trusted you.' She was so inconsolable that he began to feel quite sorry for her as she sat there with her hair down in her eyes, the picture of injured innocence.

But every time she looked up at him, he was unshakably minded of that little sharp eyed snake down in the alders. He was no longer too worried about the niceties and made to move off.

She reared up with a hiss and a tail flicked about the hem of her petticoat. 'You won't get away from me like that,' she screamed. 'I'll have you shamed in every parish in the countryside. Father!'

The drummer felt a thump on his behind. He was knocked off

121

his feet and pitched head long into an empty byre.

He peered out of a crack in the door. There was nothing to see but an old billy goat with narrow yellow eyes. He lay back and watched a golden sunbeam coming through a narrow wood-knot, marking off the hours of the summer evening as it climbed higher and higher up the wall until it blinked out.

As night fell, a voice called softly through the wall and he saw a darker shadow cross the knot-hole. 'Hush, the old man is sleeping just outside.' He knew by the sound that it was the shy girl with the chestnut hair. 'All you need to do is say that you know Snake-eyes has had a lover before, or they wouldn't be in such a rush to have her married off. The homestead in the Blue Mountains is mine; tell the old man it was me, Brandi, you were after. Hush, here he comes.' And she flitted away.

But when the shadow fell across the little hole it was the wrynecked girl who peered in. 'Are you awake, boy? Snake-eyes has you for a fool. She's mean, and she bites. The homestead in the West is mine. When I play, the gates in the mountains fly open to reveal the way into the heart of nature and all her powers. Tell them it was Randi you wanted for her song. Hush! he's stirring' she put a finger to her lips and was gone.

A little after, the hole went dark again and he heard the voices of the crow black girl. 'If my skirts hadn't been caught up, you'd have seen such a dance on the green today. The homestead in the mountains is mine by right. Tell the old man you love Gyri for her dancing feet and that you ran only to join her in a jig.' Forgetting the old man, she clapped her hands, then stole away, full of fear.

The boy sat on and as he watched the thin new moon rise, thought that he'd never been in such a corner. He'd run, but from time to time a scratching at the door reminded him that the old man slept on out there and kept watch.

'Are you there, boy?' It was the girl on the rock. 'For three hundred years I've blown my horn every summer evening here in the Blue Mountains. Many a fool has answered, but know that everything here is illusion and fatal glamour. Gunna won't be the last married. Rather than let any of them have you, I'll set you free. Listen, now when the sun is up again the old man will take to the shadows. Push hard against the door and run. Jump the fence and you're rid of us.'

The moment the sun began to burn again the drummer boy

followed her word and fled. He cleared the fence and in no time was in the valley once more. Far away, he could hear the horn call. But he slung his drum over his shoulder and set his way for Moen and the manoeuvres. Never again did he drum for the girls of the farmsteads just in case he found himself in the Blue Mountains of the West before his time.

Isaac and the Priest

T here was once a fisherman called Isaac, who lived up in Helgeland. One day, while he was out fishing for halibut, he felt something tug at his hook. He drew in the line and there on the end of it was a sea-boot.

'That's odd', he said.

He sat for a long time staring at the boot, which looked very like one of his brother's, the same brother who had been drowned in the great storm last winter on his way back from the fishing and never found. He didn't really know what to do with the thing. (He knew he didn't want to look inside, for there was definitely something in there.) If he took the boot home, he'd only upset his mother. On the other hand, since it was certainly his brother's, he didn't much feel like just chucking it back in.

At last he thought that he might ask the priest to give it a proper burial.

'I can't bury just a boot', said the priest.

'Suppose not', said Isaac. But then he wanted to know how much of a person there had to be left for a Christian burial.

'I really can't say' said the priest. 'A tooth or a finger or a lock of hair won't do. There would have to be more than that to persuade me that the soul was still present. I'll certainly not use the burial service over some old toe in a sea-boot'.

Even so, Isaac managed, on the fly, to get it buried in the churchyard. He went home, feeling he'd at least done his best. Better that something of his brother should be at rest by God's house than be flung back into the dark sea.

Later that same autumn, as he lay to off the skerries hunting seals, he brought up on his oar from among the tangles of seaweed a knife-belt and an empty sheath. Though the tarred leather had started to fall apart and though it was bleached white by the sea,

124

Isaac remembered it as his brother's.

He could even remember the day it was made; they had sat talking as his brother cut the sheath from the skin of an old horse they'd just had to slaughter. They'd bought the buckle that same Saturday over at the store where Mother sold her cloudberries and grouse and those three pounds of wool-yarn. On the way home they'd had a bit too much to drink and had stopped to tease the daft old biddy who lived up on the headland, who used her hearth-mat for a sail.

He took the belt home and said nothing. No point in causing any more sorrow, he thought. But as the winter dragged on, he found himself wondering more and more about the priest's words. What would he do if he came across another boot, or something that the squids or the crabs had been at, or something that had been snapped off by one of the fierce Greenland sharks?

He could hardly bear any longer to row the stretch of water round the skerries. Yet he was forever being drawn to that very place by the thought of finding something else, something big enough still to have a soul in it, big enough for a Christian burial.

The thought haunted him throughout the day. He stood for hours without doing a hand's turn, staring into space. Even at home, at night, he had bad dreams. When the wind crashed the door open with a sudden damp chill, it would seem as if his brother had come back and was stumping round the room demanding his missing foot back.

It got so he thought he was going completely mad. And he blamed himself for having that foot buried in the churchyard. Either way, it seemed, whether he threw it back or left it there on its own, his brother seemed trapped in limbo. Isaac couldn't close his eyes without imagining all the things that might be drifting and tossing to and fro out there among the skerries.

And so he took to dragging with ropes and fishing gear. But all he ever brought up was weed and wrack, starfish, nothing. One evening as he sat out there, he cast a line loaded with weights and hooks. The very last hook caught his left eye, and down to the bottom it went. Since there was little point in searching, he went home without it.

That night, unable to sleep for the pain, he lay in the dark, holding a bandage over the empty socket, thinking no-one in the world could possibly have so little luck. Suddenly everything went strange. He seemed to be at the bottom of the sea, looking about him as the fish clustered round the fishing line. They snapped at the bait and then wriggled as they tried to get free. First came a cod, then a ling, then a coley. Then a haddock which mumbled at the water before swallowing the bait. Then his eye was caught by something else: a man's back, with one leather sleeve caught under a grappling iron. Just at that moment, a huge pale halibut snapped at the last hook and everything went dark again.

He could now hear a voice: 'This hook is tearing at my mouth. When you catch the big halibut tomorrow, please throw it back again. But there's no good searching except at the turn of the evening tide'.

The next day, Isaac weighted his line with a lump of gravestone from the churchyard; that evening, with the tide on the turn, he lay out in the sound again. He did as he was bid and threw back the halibut. Almost at once he drew in a boat's grappling iron, with a leather jerkin caught in the flukes. The fish had been busy on the remains of an arm, nibbling as far as they could inside the sleeve.

Isaac rowed off to find the priest.

'You're honestly asking me to read the burial service over some sodden sea-jacket', roared the old man.

'I'd throw in the boot as well.'

'But I can't just throw the church's consecrated soil to the four winds', said the priest, getting angrier by the moment.

Isaac looked him straight in the eyes. 'That boot has been a sore enough burden without having to sort out a leather jacket as well.'

'Then announce it as salvage or lost property on the church board', bellowed the priest and slammed the door behind him.

'I suppose so', said Isaac, and went off home.

But he got neither peace nor rest, with the weight that lay upon him. At night, he saw the great white halibut swimming round in a circle as if held by an invisible net. He'd watch it nosing at the unseen mesh for hours until his blind eye pained him again.

Now, as soon as he went out dredging, a great ugly squid would come along and blacken the water with its ink. So one evening he just allowed the boat to drift as the current took it, out beyond the skerries offshore but still in the lee of the larger islands. At last it came to a stop as though it were anchored. Everything went quiet, not a bird-cry, not a fish-splash. Until, all at once, a huge bubble wobbled up from the depths close by an oar and burst with a heavy sigh.

From that day onward, it was said that Isaac had the second sight and saw things that were hidden from others. He could tell where the fish were and where the waters were empty. And if you asked him how he knew, he would say, 'I don't know, but my brother does'.

One day, it so happened that the priest was called out along the coast. Isaac was asked to help crew the boat, as was the custom for the men in the area. They set off in a good brisk wind, the priest got there safely and finished up his business as fast as he could.

'The fjord looks rough to me', he said, 'and it's coming on dark. But I suppose since we got here all right, there won't be any problem getting back. I hope not, for there's a service in the morning'.

But they hadn't got very far before a storm blew up and they had to slacken the sail. The waves were as big as houses and spray and sleet whipped about their ears. The priest had never seen the like. As they sailed on, night fell. The sea shone like a glacier and the gusts were stronger than ever. Isaac had just taken in another reef on the sail when a plank was sprung and the sea came pouring into the boat. In a panic, the priest and crew jumped up on the gunwale, shouting that they were lost.

'I don't believe there's anything to worry about', said Isaac, calmly taking the tiller.

And as the moon glowed fitfully through the sleet, they saw a strange boatman in the scuppers bailing every bit as fast as the water coming in.

'I don't recall hiring that man', said the priest. 'And what's he bailing with? It looks like a sea-boot. There isn't any flesh on his legs and why does his jacket flap empty?'

'I think the minister knows who it is', said Isaac.

'By the authority of my holy office', said the priest, getting angry again, 'I call on him to leave this boat'.

'Fair enough', said Isaac, 'but does your reverence know how to fix that plank?'

At that, the priest fell silent for a bit. 'Well, he does look very strong and we are in great peril. It's no sin to help a servant of God over the sea. But what does he want for his hire?'

'Only three shovelfuls of earth on an old sea-boot and a rotten leather jerkin', replied Isaac.

'The soul must still be present, else you wouldn't come to haunt us like this. There's still room for you in heaven and you shall have your drop of earth.'

The priest had bellowed his promise against the wind but at his words the water fell smooth and the boat fetched up on the sand with a jolt that snapped its cross-tree, but otherwise safe and sound.

Finn Blood

Up in Svartfjord, just north of Senje, there lived a lad called
Eilert. There was little love lost between his family and their
neighbours, who were Finns, for the fishing banks round there
were only large enough for one good boat.

Though his parents didn't like it — and often tried to stop him
— Eilert spent much of his time over with the Finns, who lived on
the far side of the headland, below the crags. They were great
story-tellers and Eilert heard marvellous things about the caverns
of the old Finn-kings, the master-magicians of olden times. And
he heard, too, of the Merman and the Sea-Ghosts, stories of evil
powers that made his blood freeze in his veins.

The Finns told him how the Sea-Ghost would show itself on
the beach by moonlight, looming from those dark spots where
seaweed gathers. Its hair was made of wrack and its head was
shaped so strangely that whoever was confronted by it couldn't help
but look into its pale, ghastly face. The Finns had seen it many a
time, they said, and once had even to drive the thing out of their
boat. Eilert hurried home that night, skirting the piles of seaweed,
afraid to look behind him.

Things got worse between the families and much was said out
of turn. Eilert got used to hearing ill of his friends. They either
couldn't row, or rowed like women, high and fast. And, like the
women, they talked and scared the fish. Not least, they practised
the black arts and worshipped stones.

All this, and the oft-repeated whisper: that to have Finnish
blood in your veins was the worst possible shame. The Finns were
not as good as others. The council had given them their own
corner of the Svartfjord churchyard and their own murky pews out
of sight of the pulpit. The rest was hearsay but this Eilert *had* seen.

And it made him angry, for he liked the Finns, especially little

129

Zilla, a pale girl with black hair and big eyes, who knew all there
was to know about the Merman. Eilert and she were inseparable,
but something nagged at him while they played. For as she gazed
at him, telling her tales, it would come back to mind that she and
all her people were among the damned. That was where their
knowledge came from.

Even so, he could still feel angry at their mistreatment. Zilla
couldn't understand these changes in his mood but she laughed
him out of it and danced off to some new hiding place.

One day he came across her sitting on a rock on the beach. In
her lap there was an eider duck, newly dead, still warm. It was, she
cried, the very bird that built its nest in their boat-shed. She knew
it by the odd red feather in its breast. This was now matched by a
bullet wound, just one, from which there had come one large drop
of blood. The bird, she said, had been trying to get home, but had
died here on the beach.

Eilert laughed as boys do, but his heart wasn't behind it and that
showed in his pale face. For that very day he had taken a pot with
his father's gun at an eider that was swimming way out beyond the
surf. He kept his mouth shut and from beneath his brows watched
her dry her tears with her hair in that wild Finnish way she had.

That autumn, Eilert's father was getting desperate. Day after
day his lines were coming up empty, while the Finns drew in
boatloads. He had to pretend not to notice the mocking gestures
from their boat. But all this did was to heap up the bitterness. And
the suspicions, for there was no question, something was at work.
Wisdom had it there was only one remedy and that was to rub
grave-soil on the lines, but this was a fearful thing to do. The dead
took quick offence and could yield you up to the power of the sea-
folk.

All this preyed on Eilert's mind, for it seemed to him that again
he was to blame, being such a friend of the Finns. The next
Sunday, when they were all at church, he quietly pocketed a clod
of earth from one of the Finnish graves, over by the corner. And
that evening, back home, he smeared the clay all over his father's
lines. The very next day, sure enough, the catches were as good as
they'd ever been.

But even so, Eilert was very far from happy. In the evenings, as
they sat mending nets round the fire, he looked uneasily into the
dark corners of the kitchen, fingering the talisman in his pocket.

There is only one way to be sure of avoiding the dead's revenge and that is by asking their forgiveness. Otherwise, they come for you in the night, dragging you off to the churchyard with invisible hands that can unpick the tightest of locks.

And so, when Eilert next went to church, he took particular care to visit the same grave and ask its owner's pardon.

As he got older, Eilert began to doubt the idea that the Finns were of a truly different sort but he did come to believe that they must represent some poorer line of stock than his own people.

He still went about with Zilla and they spent many hours together, especially round their confirmation time. But, as Eilert grew into a man, and met more and more of the local people in the daily round, he couldn't avoid the feeling that his friendship with the girl lowered him in their eyes. People *did* still think there was something shameful in Finnish blood and Eilert found himself trying to avoid her when others were around.

The girl understood well enough and learned to keep out of his road. Even so, one day she came down to the house (as she'd done often enough before) to beg a seat in their boat for church the following morning. There were strangers from the village in the room and so, lest anyone think they were courting or anything, Eilert told her she must find someone else to row her across, and added cruelly to the others 'Though I suppose a little church-going would not go amiss. Might help to curb all that witchcraft.'

Zilla left without another word and Eilert's brave good humour faded with the closing of the door.

One winter's day thereafter he was out on his own spinning for shark. He got a sudden bite, a fierce Greenland shark; his boat was small and the fish was very strong. As the struggle went on into the twilight, the boat capsized.

All night Eilert lay on the upturned keel, soaked with mist and spray. Almost fainting with tiredness, dimly aware (and not much caring, to be truthful) that the end could not be far off, he suddenly saw a figure in sea-clothes sitting astride the keel up by the bow, glaring at Eilert with dully glowing red eyes.

The man — if man it was — was so heavy that the boat began to sink at the bow. Then the figure vanished and it seemed to Eilert that the fog started to life; the sea fell completely calm, not the faintest swell, and there in front of the drifting boat was a little low islet.

131

It was greyly wet, as if the sea had just broken over it, and on it stood a lovely young girl, pale skinned and with large soft eyes. She wore a green robe and round her waist a broad silver belt covered in those figures the Finns use. Her tunic was of brownish hide and beneath its laces (which seemed to be of sea-grass) with a pure white bodice, like the down of a sea-bird.

As the boat bumped against the islet she stepped forward with a welcoming smile, almost as if she knew him well. If there was any doubt about her expression, her words made it clear, 'You've been so long, Eilert! I've been waiting for you.'

An icy chill went through him as he took her hand and stepped ashore. But it passed. In the middle of the island he could see an opening from which a flight of brassy steps led down to a cabin. As he stood looking about him, he saw two huge dogfish — at least thirty feet long — circling nearby. The girl led him to the steps and as they descended, the dogfish sank down too, one on each side. With a start, Eilert realised that the island was made of some heavy, greyish glass. The girl saw that he was afraid and told him that the fish were only her father's guards. The old man was waiting below and Eilert wasn't to be put off by his appearance, which wasn't exactly handsome but wasn't to be feared either.

Eilert now realised he was actually under water though there was no sensation of wetness. He walked on the white sandy bottom, kicking up white, red, blue and silver shells. He could see thickets of sea-grass and in the distance whole mountains covered in wrack and weed. On every side, fish darted about, just as above sea-birds wheel round the rocks.

As they walked along she explained things to him. High above he could see a dark shape, like a cloud with a lighter lining. Beneath it, to and fro, there moved a form like one of the dogfish.

'That's a boat', said the girl, 'and the other is your friend, who visited you last night and shared your keel. There's dirty weather up there and if that one sinks there will be work to do and father won't have time for you today.' As she turned back, there was a fierce gleam in her eye which almost immediately faded back into a smile.

It wasn't easy to read those eyes. As a rule, they were heavy and glowing, like sea-fire in a wave. But when she laughed, they turned a bright green, like the sun slanting through shallows.

Now and then they passed a boat half buried in the sand, fish soaring through the cabin doors or roosting (as it looked) in the windows. Round the hulks wandered human shapes no more solid than blue smoke. Eilert's guide explained that these were the spirits of drowned men who had not had a Christian burial. These were the half-dead, to be avoided. They could feel a coming wreck in their hollow bones and at such times howled their death-warnings through the windy night.

They moved on across a deep shaded valley. Among the rocks above his head Eilert could see a row of white doors from which there came a glow like that of the Northern Lights in the autumn sky. His companion told him that the valley jutted right under the land and that inside each door there lived one of the old Finn-kings who had died at sea.

She opened the nearest. There on a plinth of stone sat a wrinkled, yellow-skinned old man with rheumy eyes and a dark-red gleaming crown. He was the last of the kings, drowned in a storm he had called up but couldn't calm again. His old head rocked back and forth on his skinny neck, like a band of weed in an ocean current.

Beside him on the block was a tiny shrivelled woman, wearing a crown, her clothes studded with coloured stones. She was stirring something over a pile of cold sticks. If only she had fire, the girl said, the old king and queen would soon rule again over the disobedient sea. But the potion was cold.

A plain opened up at a turn in the valley. On it stood a little town and a church, upside down, as if mirrored in glass. The girl explained that this was her father's home and that the spired church was one of seven in his kingdom, which stretched all over the north lands.

No service had ever been held there because the drowned bishop could not remember the name of the Lord he served. He and his congregation of Sea-Ghosts could do nothing but rack their brains. The bishop had been here for 800 years and so an answer couldn't be far off. A century back, they'd sent one of the Sea-Ghosts up to the church at Rödö to find out, but every time the name was mentioned, he couldn't catch the sound of it.

In a cave on Mt Kunna old King Olav had hung a bell of pure gold, guarded by the first priest of Nordland dressed in a white robe. On the day the priest rings the bell, Kunnan will be turned into a huge stone church and all the north lands, above and below the water, will be called to worship. For now, though, everyone who comes below is asked for that elusive word.

At this Eilert felt worse than ever for he realised he too had forgotten God's name. As he struggled to remember, the girl looked anxiously into his face, as if willing the thought to rise to the surface. When it clearly wouldn't, she turned away, looking pale.

They arrived at the Merman's house (which the glassy effect of the water had made to appear, at first, at the foot of the steps). It was a jumble of broken keels and planks, all glued together with sea-grass and slime. Three heavy masts, snapped off and crusted with barnacles, formed the door posts and lintel; the door itself was waterlogged planks, heavy with nails. In the middle, in place of a knocker, was an old mooring ring and a length of tattered hawser. As they approached, the door swung open, to be slammed behind them by a huge black arm that snaked out of the shadows.

They were in a high room with a fine grit of shell spread over the floor. All around lay bits of rope and gear, kegs and barrels, mostly empty. On a pile of hemp, covered with an old worn red sail, sat the Merman himself, a heavy figure with a sou'wester pushed back on his head, dark red matted hair and beard, small, teary shark's eyes and a smile that (like his daughter's expression) changed from good nature to hungry evil as you watched.

His head and neck were like a seal's. Hair grew thickly on the nape and the tops of his fingers were webbed. He sat there in old sea-boots with the tops turned down and with grey wool stockings pulled up over his knees. His clothes were plain worsted but there were glass buttons on his waistcoat. A jacket of skin hung open and there was an old red muffler wrapped round the thick neck.

As Eilert came in, he made to rise and called, 'Welcome, my boy, you've had a day of it! Sit down if you can find a place and take a little something. Pffft.' The squirt of tobacco juice was like a whale sounding. With a foot, which stretched out an extraordinary length, he hooked Eilert out a whale's skull to serve as a stool, in the meantime reaching behind him to drag into view a sea-chest stuffed with food. There were pots of porridge, honey cakes, smoked fish, bannocks and butter, and a whole host of dishes that would not have disgraced a captain's table.

The Merman told Eilert to eat his fill and ordered the girl to fetch the last keg of spirits. ('Last is always best', he said aside.)

When it arrived, Eilert recognized it at once by the stamp on its side; it was the very one he had bought for his father only days before for the grog-shop in Kvæford. The lad would have spoken up but something else caught his eye, for the quid of tobacco in the Merman's mouth, which he was even now awkwardly shifting around in order to get a good mouthful of drink, was exactly like the plug of lead from Eilert's line. And it was dark blood, not tobacco juice, that the Merman spat into the cold grate.

So they sat quietly, taking turns to drink until Eilert decided he'd had plenty. He passed on his next turn, saying he would rather not, at which the Merman upended the keg and drained it to the bottom. It clearly wasn't the last after all for he immediately reached up for another with that long black arm. He was in good form now, talking and laughing. This last made Eilert quail for his host's mouth yawned alarmingly wide, revealing a row of greenish, gappy fangs, like a bleached boat-frame.

The Merman followed the new keg with another still and grew very talkative indeed. He gazed all the while at Eilert as if he thought the whole thing very funny and wanted to say, 'Well, my young catch, *now* who's got who?' But all he did say was, 'You had a bad night of it, my lad, but you'd have suffered less if you hadn't caked those lines with grave-soil and if you hadn't refused my daughter a berth in your Sunday boat.' Here he stopped and muffled his mouth with the spirit keg. But Eilert caught an eye so full of hate and revenge that his back and legs trembled.

A long, bobbing swallow seemed to douse the look of evil and when the keg came down empty the Merman seemed in better mood and returned to his story-telling. He stretched out on the sail and laughed contentedly at his own jokes, most of which were about wrecks or drownings. Every now and then, Eilert caught the gust of a chuckle which, for all the spirits his host had taken, was like a chill wind. 'If people would only give up their boats. It's the wood I'm after, not the crew, but I can't do without my supply of planks and timbers. When things get low, I must have a ship or boat. Surely no-one could blame for that?'

With this, he realized the keg was empty and became sour again, telling Eilert how bad times were for him and the girl. Things weren't the way they used to be. He gazed straight ahead for a while as if thinking, then stretched himself out backwards, his feet trailing across the floor, gave a yawn that looked like a boat on the stocks, and dozed off.

At this the girl reappeared and told Eilert to follow. They took the same route back, up the brass steps to the islet. There she told him that her father had been so angry because of the cruel joke about 'witchcraft' and church-going. Eilert had been brought to see if he knew the name they sought, but she'd seen herself on the way down that the sea-magic had driven it from his head. Now he was on his own again. It would be an hour or three before the old man slept it off. Till then, Eilert must get some rest of his own while she kept watch.

The girl tossed her dark hair over him like a veil and it seemed to him as he gazed up that he knew her eyes well. He felt for a drowsing moment that his cheek was resting against the breast of a white sea-bird, a single red feather on it, melting in his tired sight even as it stirred up some deep memory. As he slipped off, he heard her lullaby, like the rhythm of the waves on the beach in summer. It told of their childhood, their games and their falling-out. Later, he could only remember the final words.

> *This is the song of my wounded breast*
> *Its salt drops kiss your brow.*
> *Who holds you now with grieving soul?*
> *Who holds you weeping now?*
>
> *Though friends we were, when we were young,*
> *Our friendship's colder now.*
> *Whose love was spurned, whose heart was torn?*
> *Who broke our unsaid vow?*
>
> *You lay in wait on our childhood beach,*
> *As home to my nest I flew.*
> *This is the wound you gave me then,*
> *This is the mark I bear of you.*

And it seemed to Eilert that she wept above him, letting salt splashes fall on his cheek. He knew now how much he loved her.

But he stirred in his dream-sleep. It seemed at that moment that a whale had come right up to the islet and that the girl told him to hurry. He stood on its back and thrust his oar down the shiny red spout-hole to stop its diving. He quickly found that he could steer, right and left, merely by twisting the oar from side to side. The land shot by at incredible speed. Behind, he could see the Merman come racing in pursuit, churning up a great wall of foam. A moment later, he seemed to wake again with the girl bent over him. 'It's me, Eilert.'

As he shook off drowsiness, it seemed they were still on the wet, sunlit islet, he and the sea-girl. But the scene gradually took shape. The sun was shining through dusty window glass. He was on a bed, under a patched red Finnish blanket, and it was Zilla who sat by his side, holding him. They had thought he was going to die, for he had been out of his head with fevers and sickness for six weeks, ever since they had rescued him from the capsized boat.

Any qualms about Finn blood were gone. That spring he and Zilla were betrothed, and married in the autumn. There were Finns, of course, in the bride's train and there was plenty talk about that along the pews. But everyone agreed that the Finnish fiddler was the best they'd ever heard and that the bride was the prettiest they'd ever seen.

The Elf-Trout

T he fish Nona had hooked was an odd one, to be sure. Big
and fat, brightly scaled and covered in red spots, it wriggled and
fought his line, struggling against the barb. When he got it into the
boat and freed it, he saw that in place of eyes it only had tiny slits.

'It must be an elf-trout', said one of the crew. 'This must be one
of those lakes with a cavern below.' Nona didn't worry overmuch
what sort of fish it was. He was hungry and wanted to eat and
talked the others into going ashore as fast as possible.

They'd been out there the whole day with empty lines, nothing,
then the fish had come along, gulp! at the bait and, there, dinner
just when you thought you were going to go without any.

Nona didn't let the strange eyes bother him till he had the thing
picked clean but for the head and fins. There were only those slits
on the outside, but as he poked his fork into them, he could feel
what seemed hard, stone-like eyeballs inside. It had tasted all
right, but he wished now he'd looked a bit closer before he'd
cooked it.

As he lay half asleep later, there was a sensation on his face like
light coming off water. He tossed and turned and thought of the
strange fish.

Suddenly, it seemed that he was back on his boat and that the
fish was in his hands again, threshing and fighting for life,
snapping its head back and forth to be free of the hook.

All at once, it seemed that the fish grew heavy as lead and drew
the boat down on the end of the line. They dived at an incredible
speed and the lake seemed to dry up as they went, sucking away
towards the point the fish headed. The boat shot into a hole like a
funnel in the lake floor and in a strange twilight began to glide
along an underground river. The air, that had been cold and
clammy, grew warmer and warmer. The splashing died down and

138

the stream flowed very gently, gradually widening until it merged with a large, calm lake.

Away on the far side, half-seen in the gloom, there were bogs and marshes and Nona could hear giant animals crashing about. Noisily, they rose and fell in the warm mud.

In the marsh-glow, he could see shoals of fish near his boat, all of them eyeless. In the distance, he caught glimpses of great sea-snakes and he realised that this was their home; it was from here that they rose to pop their heads out of the water in the summer calms, scaring the wits out of fishermen.

The great duck-worm, with its flat head and bird's beak, chased after fish and wriggled up towards the surface through the tangles of marsh-glass and mire. Through the close, muggy gloom there came, now and again, shivers of cold from off the scales of the slithering corpse-worm, that beast which bores its greenish way up through the soil and into the coffins in the churchyard.

Those creatures that haunt highland streams, the evil and pitiless water-horses, tore at their prey in the shallows, tossing their long, tangled manes.

And Nona caught sight of those half-human figures that sailors and fishermen see on rocks and that farmers find on their ricks and dungheaps.

Through all this, there was a humming in the air of invisible things, close as breathing but never solid enough to see or touch.

Then the boat drifted into a soft, slimy patch and again took a downward turn. The earth all around darkened as they sank. All at once there came a bolt of light, bright blue, from a patch high above. The air grew thick and pungent, the water round the hull as yellow and soupy as the dregs in an old iron boiler. Nona thought at once of the warm springs, with their sulphurous, poisonous water, that had spoiled many an attempt to dig a sweet well, wasting a whole day's work.

The heat was intense and boiling mud thundered and fell all around. The vapour that rose worked its way into his head. He felt as though his body were lightening, coming free and floating upward. He seemed wonderfully light and balanced, almost with the power to fly. And then, before he knew how he got there, he was on solid ground again, or at least on his old horse-hair mattress, which was almost as hard.

The Cormorants of Andvaer

Just beyond Andvær on the way north there lies an island haunted by sea-birds. No boat can land there, even in the quietest weather, for its rocks are surrounded by deadly whirlpools and rips.

There were those, though, who had seen a gleam like a large gold ring through the surf and people said there was a treasure there, from the pirate days. And at sunset sometimes, sailors would catch a glimpse through the gathering mist of an old ship sailing straight out from the wicked cliff.

The cormorants of Andvaer sit in a long black row along the rocks, waiting for dogfish. Tradition has it that there are only ever twelve of the birds on the island. But a thirteenth lives on a lonely rock out in the sound and is only seen when it rises out of the mist to fly across the island.

The only people at the summer fishing station the whole year round were a woman and a young girl. Their task, once the fishing season was over, was to guard the fish-drying racks against the hungry skuas and fulmars who swoop down to peck at the ropes, in search of morsels of fish.

The girl had thick, dark hair and strange squinty eyes. There were some who said she resembled the cormorants out there on the island and certainly she saw more of them than of human folk. No-one knew who her father was.

She grew up quickly and it soon happened that the fisher-lads began to bargain slyly for the job of collecting the dried fish from the summer station. Some offered a share of the cut, others dipped into their wages; back home in their villages more than the usual number of engagements were being broken off. The cause of it all was the dark girl with the strange eyes.

Odd as she was, and no real beauty, there was something about her. She turned the head of almost anyone who got talking to her. Pretty soon, back at work, they couldn't talk about anything else.

The first actually to propose to her had his own house and boatyard to offer. 'Come back in the summer with the right ring and we'll see', said the girl.

Sure enough, he was back with the sun and with a load of fish that would have paid for the biggest ring anyone could want. But, 'The ring I want lies over at the island, in an iron chest under the wreckage. If you love me enough, you'll go and get it.'

The young man went pale. He thought of the riptides and the breakers that throw up foam even on the gentlest days and he thought of the line of waiting cormorants.

'I love you, of course I do, but that trip would be my funeral, not my wedding.'

As he spoke, in the distance, the thirteenth cormorant rose off its stone in the mist and spray and flew over the island.

Next winter, there came a man who was steersman on a schooner. For two years now, he had nursed a secret love for her. The answer was the same. 'If you come again in summer-time and bring with you the ring I'll be married with, then I'm yours.'

Prompt on midsummer day, he reappeared at the station. But when he learned where the ring was he went off and cried, and kept crying right through the midnight sun.

And the thirteenth cormorant took flight and flapped over the island.

All through the third winter the weather was dreadful and many ships were wrecked. One stormy morning, an upturned boat drifted ashore with a young lad clinging to the keel exhausted, hanging on only by his belt. There was barely a spark of life left in him, for all the old woman's fires and poultices and broths.

As they sat by the fire, the girl suddenly started and cried out, 'It's my bridegroom'. And she held him to her breast and rocked him and put warmth in his chilling heart. By morning, he was restored.

'I dreamt I lay between the wings of a great cormorant and laid my head against its feathers', he said. He was a handsome lad, with curly hair, healthy for all his recent brush with death, and he couldn't take his eyes off his saviour.

They gave him a job at the fishing station but when it came to it he did little work, spending most of his time talking to the girl, making her laugh. And things went with him as they had with all the others. Within a month, he was convinced he could not live without her. On the day he was to go back to sea, he proposed.

'I'll tell you no lies,' she said. 'I've held you in my arms and I'd give my own life to keep you from sorrow. You can have me if you have the ring for my finger, but even then you can have me for one day only. I'll wait for you and long for you till summer comes.'

On midsummer's day the lad sailed back again and she told him of the ring she must have from the chest among the rocks.

'You pulled me from the sea and it's in your power to send me back, for I can't live without you.' As he dipped his oars to row out, she stepped down into the boat and sat in the stern. It was beautiful summer weather and there was a gentle swell on the open sea, wave after wave in quiet rhythm. The lad worked at his oars, lost in the mysteries of her face, until he heard the crash of the breakers on the island and felt the tug of its currents.

'If you love life, turn back', said the girl.

'You're more to me than life itself', he replied.

The swell was powerful close in and the foam shot up high as a steeple but just as it seemed the boat was going down and death near, they broke through into a calm and the boat drifted safely ashore.

On the beach, on the line of the tide, there was an old rusted anchor, half-buried in the shingle. 'Below that hook is an iron chest and in it my dowry. Bring it to the boat and put the ring you see on my finger. That will be our wedding and I will be yours till the sun leans toward the sea.'

It was a gold ring with a bright red stone. He put it on her hand and kissed her. They lay down in a patch of grass in the middle of the island and he felt a soaring happiness.

'Midsummer day is lovely and I am young and you are my husband. This must be our bridal bed.'

He could hardly contain his love for her.

As night drew on and the sun began to dip toward the sea, she kissed him and cried.

'The summer day is lovely and so is the summer night but my dark is coming now.'

And it seemed that she was growing older as he watched and fading before his eyes. And when the sun tipped the water there was nothing left before him but a pile of empty rags, no more.

The sea was calm and from the rocks below twelve cormorants sailed out over the water.

The Wind-Troll's Daughter

Young Captain Bardun, who lived up in Dyrevig, was a stubborn character. Once he'd set his mind to something, there was no putting him off it. If he promised to come to a dance, the girls could count on at least one partner, even if there were a gale outside, or a sudden fall of snow.

He'd come labouring up in his little boat through the roughest weather and the girls would wait to be whirled round the floor, while their boyfriends stood surly along the walls, glowering at the cocky sod.

He was a great shark fisherman and would take his boat and gaffe into waters even the biggest boats would avoid. If there was something everyone else was afraid to try, Bardun was your man for it. And, daft as the venture might be, he came out ahead every time and added yet another exploit to his reputation.

Away out beyond the skerries was a great rock, nested by duck and sea-birds. The merchant who owned it went out there every year to bring back great sackfuls of eider-down. On the side of the rock, there was a deep gully, so steep that no-one could be quite sure how far into the rock it went. It had become a saying, for something that couldn't be done, that it was as impossible as taking eider-down from Dyrevig gorge. The merchant, knowing he was quite safe, had said many a time that anyone who could gather feathers from the deep gully was welcome to them.

Bardun had heard this and had seen from the water how the birds poured in their thousands from the mouth of the gully, away from interfering hands. He made up his mind to try his luck. Just like him, he set out the very next day, in bright sunshine. He took a long rope which he wound twice or thrice round a rocky spur; then he lowered himself, swinging back and forth until he got a good foothold. Then he began to stuff his bags with the soft down.

He ranged so far into the gully that the daylight was no more than a crack of blue behind and above him. Inside, the rocks were thick with feathers and he couldn't gather the half of what was there.

It was late before he finished. When he came out, the stone that he had put on the rope end was gone and his rope hung out of reach, dangling over the sheer drop. The wind blew it about madly but always kept it away from his stretching hand. He tried again and again to reach it, until the sun began to sink down towards the water.

He was wakened, in full light again and with a changed breeze, by a voice from somewhere above his head.

'It blows away, it blows away.'

He looked up and saw a big woman shaking the rope, holding it away from the cave mouth. Each time he grabbed at it, she flicked it out of reach of his fingers, grinning and laughing with a voice that echoed across the hillside.

'It blows away, it blows away.'

And the rope danced to and fro.

'Well', thought Bardun, 'if I'm to make a jump for it, it better be now, not when I'm tired.'

It was a fair distance but he took a good run at it and leapt out over the drop. Not like Bardun to fall short! He caught the rope and clung on. To his surprise, he began to move up the cliff-face, almost as if he were being hoisted.

When he reached the rocky spur where he'd tied the top end, he heard a whispering and a sighing. 'I am the daughter of the Wind-Troll, and now I'm yours. The wind that blows round you now and in future will be my breaths of love. At your feet lies a rudder that will give you luck and a good bearing wherever you want to sail. Your friends will prosper, your enemies will suffer shipwreck and ruin. I control the winds.'

All at once, everything fell still round him, though at sea he could still see the squalls blowing. He picked up the rudder and made certain not to leave it behind when he loaded his boat.

He sailed off with a racing breeze behind him and soon met a schooner bound for Bergen whose captain gave him top price for the sacks of down.

Bardun knew a good thing when he saw it and went back to Dyrevig rock many times, piling sacks of feathers half-way up to his mast. Business prospered; he bought ships and houses and, in due course, whole fishing grounds, up north and in southern waters, both.

His clients (those at least who accepted his advice) did every bit as well. Those who ignored or thwarted him met with disaster; the last thing they heard, as the water closed over their heads, was the loving whisper of the Wind-Troll's daughter, uttering Bardun's name.

Things were going pretty well. What was ruin to others was success to him. He soon controlled all the fishing-stations up in Finnmark and even had his interests away up in Spitzbergen, amid the ice. No-one could sell their fish up there without his leave and even down in Bergen half the ships in the harbour bore his mark. He did whatever suited him, but expected others to do his bidding.

The magistrates came to think he had too much power for one man and they began to make inquiries among the people Bardun had bossed about for so long. And, in due course, they sent him a warning.

'That rudder is *my* magistrate's rod', thought Bardun to himself, and ignored their summons.

At last things got to such a pass that the council set out to arrest him. No sooner were they on the sea than a storm blew up out of nowhere. Down they went into the icy water.

As a stopgap, until the king could appoint new men, Bardun was made chief magistrate. The replacement, when his name came through, quickly came to the unhappy conclusion that though Bardun had handed back the job without a fuss, he still expected to run things. For all the new chief's letters of appointment, there was only one boss.

History repeated itself. Bardun was summoned. When he failed to respond, the magistrates set out to arrest him. Ten minutes out of harbour, they went down in an unexpected storm.

When the next governor was appointed, nothing of him arrived but the broken keel of his ship. After that, they got the message and Bardun was left to rule over all. In the north country, he was like the king himself.

He had only one child, a daughter called Boel. She was tall and as lovely as the sun. None of the young men were good enough for her, though she hinted that she'd be glad enough to see a prince on his knees before her.

Suitors came from all over the place, but were sent away. The dowry was to be enormous, the biggest ever heard of in that land, but none of the young men matched up.

One year a young officer came north with papers from the king. His uniform was heavy with gold braid that shone and sparkled in the light. Bardun was glad to see him and together they worked on replies to the king. The best thing was to come, though, and the best thing Bardun had heard since his own wife had accepted him. For Boel came to say that the young officer had proposed and that if she weren't allowed to marry him she'd throw herself into the sea in his wake.

Bardun was delighted for now he could see his line go on after he was dead. That summer, while the officer was still on his circuit, Bardun set a hundred men to building a house for the young couple. It was to be like a castle, high and light, with halls and dance-rooms, hung and carpeted with the best materials from the south.

That autumn there was a wedding that was the talk of the whole land. Soon after, Bardun discovered that there was talk of something else, and that it was true. His son-in-law, as people had said, was another man who expected his way in all things. He spoke his mind and more than once over-ruled Bardun himself.

He went to his daughter and told her to bring her husband to heel, and quickly. The honeymoon was not yet over and no young husband would fail to obey his bride's wishes. But Boel said she'd married no less a man than Bardun himself and that her husband spoke with the king's authority.

So Bardun decided to bide his time and make the best of things. It's easy enough to get round the young if you only let them believe they're getting their own way. Whatever was amiss, he'd soon be able to put it right.

He praised everything his son-in-law did and built him up endlessly in people's eyes, telling them he was glad to have such an able man to take his place when he was gone. And at this he'd hunch his back and quaver his voice as if he were already well past it. But it didn't escape Boel how he slammed about the place striking angry sparks from the cobbles with his boots and stick.

The next time the court met, Bardun was told he had to pay in tax a full tenth of his possessions, as was the law but as he'd failed to do in the past when there was no-one to force him. This time, he drew only a little surly comfort from the fate of magistrates in the past.

All women like show, he knew. Was Boel any different? (Well, he thought, she was his daughter and should be able to keep the upper hand of her husband without bribes.) Even so, he tried to turn her head with gold and jewels, one day a bangle, the next a chain or a belt or gold-stitched shoes. And he told her that she was the richest jewel of all; everything else in the world was dull by comparison.

And then he hinted that she might change her husband's mind about this or that piece of business. All to no avail. Things got steadily harder for Bardun. The king's word (as delivered by his son-in-law) came first; his wishes lagged behind.

He began to fear the outcome and his temper kept people well clear of him. His eyes burned and at night he'd pace up and down, shouting at Boel and calling her every kind of terrible thing.

One morning, after one of these outbursts, he came in to her with a heavy gold crown full of precious jewels. If she could rule her husband, she'd be queen of the north, he promised.

Boel looked coldly at him and said that she would never betry her husband into breaking the king's law. At this Bradun went as pale as parchment and hurled the crown against the wall, showering them both with stones and shivers of glass.

'I, and no other, am king here!' he roared and spat threats at those like her husband who sought to take his power away.

Boel swore to have no more to do with her father and warned her husband that they ought to leave. Three days later, they packed up all the wedding gifts and sailed away.

Bardun was frantic and dashed his head against the wall, screaming at such a pitch that it could be heard at the quayside, laughing at his victory (for he was alone again), crying for his daughter.

That night the storm came up. The sea stayed white for a week and it was not long before news came that Boel and her husband had drowned and that the wedding clothes floated in the surf round the skerries.

Bardun took the rudder the Wind-Troll's daughter had given him and fitted it to the largest boat in his fleet. He was God Himself now, he cried, the winds obeyed him and he could rule wherever he pleased. He set sail in a fresh breeze with the waves rolling after him. The sea grew heavier, curling up into steep walls like grey cliffsides topped with feathery white. Impossible for any other boat but just the thing for a man who was to rule the whole world.

He set his rudder southwards and never slackened his sail one inch, even as the seas grew higher and higher in the wind's frenzy. And as the sea towered up he steered, fully sailed and with a whisper in his ear, straight into the sun.

Other Stories from Scandinavia
Published by Forest Books

Preparations for Flight
& Other Swedish Stories

Translated by Robin Fulton

Robin Fulton, one of the best-known translators of contemporary Swedish literature, has gathered a collection of stories which, as he says in his preface, remained in his mind long after a first reading. In all of them, concrete reality evokes mystery, and in many of them, childhood reflections affect and are affected by everyday adult experience.

ISBN 0 948259 66 3   paper £8.95   176pp

Heartwork

by Solveig von Schoultz

Translated from the Swedish
by Marlaine Delargy & Joan Tate

Winner of numerous literary prizes, Solveig von Schoultz is widely acknowledged as one of Finland's leading poets and prose writers. 'Her short stories', writes Bo Carpelan, present an acute and subtle analysis of human relationships — between adults and children, men and women, and between different generations . . . She is not only a listener and an observer: she is also passionately involved with these dramas of everyday life which are all concerned with the problems of human value and human growth. These she portrays without sentimentality but with the rich perception of experience.'

ISBN 0 948259 60 7   paper £7.95   144pp

Due December 1990:
Hour of the Lynx
A play by Per Olov Enquist

Poetry from Scandinavia
Published by Forest Books

SNOW AND SUMMERS

by Solveig von Schoultz

Translated from the Swedish by Anne Born

Snow and Summers presents the cream of von Schoultz's poetry from almost fifty years for the first time in English. 'For both poet and reader', writes Bo Carpelan, 'von Schoultz's poetry is an exercise in the sharpening of vision . . . sincerity and smiling wisdom engendered by a lifetime of experience.'

ISBN 0 948259   paper £7.95   128pp

ROOM WITHOUT WALLS

Selected poems of Bo Carpelan

Translated from the Swedish by Anne Born

Perhaps the greatest poet writing in Finland today, Bo Carpelan takes much of his inspiration from the landscape of Finland, its stern northern wintry presence and its delicate spring and summer. In style concise, pure and clear, in form economical, he writes with a delicate lyrical beauty of fundamental human experience. Beneath the spare, deceptively simple surface lie vast eternities, gentle echoes, mysteries, sorrows, signs and warnings.

ISBN 0 948259 08 6   paper £6.95   144pp illustrated

Due July 1990:
ENCHANTING BEASTS
An anthology of Finnish Women Poets
edited by Kirsti Simonsuuri